CRU

LAND

Published under licence by Brown Dog Books and
The Self-Publishing Partnership Ltd, 10b Greenway Farm,
Bath Rd, Wick, nr. Bath BS30 5RL, UK

www.selfpublishingpartnership.co.uk

ISBN printed book: 978-1-83952-873-6
ISBN e-book: 978-1-83952-874-3

Cover design by Kevin Rylands
Internal design by Richard Powell

Printed and bound in the UK

This book is printed on FSC® certified paper

MIX
Paper | Supporting
responsible forestry
FSC
www.fsc.org   FSC® C013604

CRUSOE LAND

G PAUL PLENTY

BROWN DOG BOOKS

CRUSOE
LAND

© PAUL FLEWITT

1

S am had a secret. He'd have loved to tell someone, to share the knowledge, if nothing else rather than have it bottled up inside. However, he knew that no one would believe him and even if they did, well, the consequences would be unimaginable. Perhaps it would be best if he kept quiet.

He thought he heard a click and looked round towards the gate in the churchyard wall. Behind him stood St. Michael's, a little grey stone church, with its stumpy tower that looked too small to accommodate anything but the smallest of bells. Tall trees in full green leaf, with sunlight sparkling through the gaps clustered behind the church. There was no one there.

Lying on the warm, pale stone of an ancient tombstone, the carved names and dates of the deceased all but illegible due to the passage of time, Sam stared up into the golden afternoon sunlight that seemed to flow from a cloudless blue sky. He shaded his eyes and followed the flight of a Kite that wheeled high above on the thermals rising up from the dry land. The small churchyard was overgrown with straggling grass. Hedge parsley, red poppies and the white petals of daisies spread out a splash of colour. A large bee droned nearby, energetically working away on a clump of old lavender. Sam closed his eyes and tried to stop thoughts rumbling around in his mind. Just relax in the peace and quiet of the day, he told himself. A gentle movement of air, bringing a waft of the scent of grass being cut a few fields away. Was it possible to float? To live in this moment forever, with no thoughts urging action, decisions to be made and problems solved. Sam searched again for the Kite, but it had gone and he knew that this idyllic moment was just that, a moment. Prayers were never answered, which was an odd thing in a place like this. Suddenly, Sam saw a woman slip quietly through the gate. She was tall and long golden hair framed a delicate elfin-like pale face. Wide open blue eyes regarded Sam warily. Sunlight shone from behind her cotton print dress and he couldn't help but notice the outline of long, slim legs beneath the fabric. To his eyes, she was a vision of loveliness and he blinked, as if unsure that what he saw was real. Sam gave a shy smile as she closed the gate behind her and passed out into the road. He wasn't sure if she had really seen him. The vision seemed unhappy and had what looked like a dark mark on the side of her face.

It was no good, he would have to move and go back across the road to the cottage. Happy moments always seemed to be over in a flash, whereas unpleasant ones tended to linger, Sam reflected. He rose a little stiffly and noticed that the sun was moving inexorably across the blue heavens towards the west. As he passed by, Sam glanced down at the polished grey granite tombstone of Ivan Olive that was in remarkably good condition for having been erected in the 1920s. Why call your child Ivan? Had the boy had been teased at school because of his name? Just before the gate, under the shade of an ancient yew was the standard form of Services headstone commemorating Stoker Bull RN, who had drowned at Portsmouth in December 1918 when he had fallen from his ship. It always made Sam think when he passed the stone. Fancy having survived the war, to have died in such a sad, pointless accident.

A movement out of the corner of his eye. Sam turned his head and saw Jack Price's big black tom cat emerge from under the hedge and stroll across the lawn.

'Yes, you bugger,' Sam muttered. 'You crap on the grass again and I'll give you something to remember.' The cat stopped and stared at Sam.

'Go on, sod off,' Sam hissed. Then he saw her again. A little way beyond the garden hedge, standing in the road, looking at him. A momentary gasp and a tight feeling in his chest and for a second Sam had thought it was Ellie. But no, she'd left him months ago. Unlike the previous day, the vision in the road wore denim shorts and a brilliant white plain T shirt. Sam stole a glance at the slim, tanned legs and thought he saw a bruise on a calf muscle. This time, large sunglasses helped to partially obscure the mark on her face.

'Um, can I help you?' Sam asked as the vision continued to stand still. She gave a brief smile.

'I, ah, came on the off chance. Mr Darking said he would lend me a book of his, on local history. It was a while ago.' Sam liked the light, clear sound of her voice.

'Sorry, maybe you haven't heard?' Sam said quietly. 'Mr Darking, Alec, was my uncle. He died eight weeks ago. Very sudden. Undiagnosed heart condition apparently.'

The woman gasped and raised a hand to cover her mouth.

'I'm so sorry to hear that. I didn't know.' Her shoulders seemed to sag a little and she stood still, as if unable to think what to do next.

'I haven't been about for the last couple of months.' The woman spread her hands. 'I'm really, very sorry to hear that about Alec.'

'I'm sorry to have to tell you,' said Sam. 'I can see that it's been a surprise to you. Would you like to come in for a tea, or a coffee … or something stronger?'

The woman looked about her. 'I don't suppose I could have some water please? It's been so hot today.'

'Yes, of course. Do come in.' Sam nodded towards the small gate that gave onto the road. The cat sat on the lawn, regarding Sam with disdain.

'Go on, clear off,' Sam said

'Oh dear. I've only just arrived.' The woman gave a small laugh.

'No, not you. It's Price's wretched cat. I'm sure he sends it over here to perform.'

'Don't worry, I know what you mean. When I was small, at home, I used to sneak out with a trowel and flick the offerings over Mr

Iverson's garden, preferably onto his lettuce patch. Since it was his cat, I thought it only fair.'

Sam grinned.

'Now, water you said. I think I have some elderflower cordial if you would prefer?'

'Lovely, haven't had any for a very long time.'

Sam indicated a deckchair on the lawn. 'Do sit down and I'll bring it out.'

'Thank you. By the way, I'm Juno Randall.'

'Sorry.' Sam blushed. 'I should have said. I'm Sam Darking.'

'Alec was your uncle you said?'

'Yes, I've come to sort the place out.' Sam pointed towards the long, low stone cottage that tried to hide from the road behind wide hedges.

'I've visited before. Alec was very kind,' said Juno. 'Last time I came was in November, when it was very cold. We made toast on a fork in front of the fire, with butter and, I think, homemade raspberry jam.' Juno fell silent, as if looking inwards at her store of memories. They sat quietly, sipping their drinks. Sam tried not to look too much at Juno as she gazed out over the wide open fields beyond the garden hedges. He thought she looked gorgeous, but when Juno turned her head towards him, he detected a glimpse of something … missing. A lifeless look in her eyes perhaps? Then there was the mark on the side of her face that he had noticed the day before. It looked like a bruise although Juno appeared to have applied some makeup to try and hide the blemish.

'I don't think I've seen you before yesterday … in the churchyard,' said Sam to make conversation.

'You were there?' Juno looked surprised. 'I don't remember seeing you.'

'I was relaxing on old John Buckler's tomb, soaking up the sun.'

'I'd just popped into the church for a bit of peace and of course it's cool inside.'

'Do you live locally?' Sam asked.

'Yes, in Burton House.' Juno waved a hand in the vague direction of a large, red brick Victorian villa that stood at the edge of the village, set back from the road behind a tall beech hedge and large mature chestnut trees. Sam could make out several ornate chimneys topping a large, ruddy brown tiled roof.

'Do you think you'll live here?' Juno asked.

Sam looked up at Glebe Cottage, for so long Uncle Alec's home.

'Hadn't thought that far. There's a lot to do. Sorting things out. You wouldn't believe the amount of old newspapers, magazines and books I've found tucked away. I even came across a round leather case that contained detachable wing collars. Can you believe it? Why hang on to ancient stuff like that? Not to mention two bowler hats and two commodes. Lord knows what Alec was doing with such old rubbish.'

Sam noticed that Juno was regarding him with those big blue eyes of hers, but he wasn't sure that she was looking at him, or through him. He felt a little uneasy. The sound of a car going by in the road came to disturb the peace. Sam looked over the hedge and saw a large red sports car, sending up a cloud of dust as it headed for the village. Juno sat bolt upright; a hand raised to her mouth.

'I must go,' she announced. 'Thank you for the drink.'

'Anytime,' said Sam, as he got up to show her out. 'Call in when you're about.'

2

Next morning, Sam went out early and began a half-hearted attempt to cut back some overgrown shrubs and weeds that sprouted on the gravelled paths. Thinking that this could take forever, he changed his mind and ran the electric mower over the lawn, that was badly in need of a cut. As he worked, Sam reflected upon Juno. She was all too obviously stunning to look at, but there was something else, perhaps sadness, or something guarded, he couldn't put his finger on it after such a short acquaintance. Sam had hoped old Price might come creeping along the road that ran the short distance into Sheriford. The village was fortunate enough to be still served by a shop-cum-Post Office and Sam knew that Price usually walked along from his house, just over and down from Glebe Cottage to buy a newspaper. Just for exercise, Price had once said. Not, he had grumbled, that there was anything worth reading in the papers these days. Country's gone to the dogs was Price's favourite moan. He put Sam in mind of a character called The Barfly, who used to be always sitting at the King's Head pub, which Sam frequented when he lived with Ellie. The old guy, with his watery eyes, puffy veined face and the ruddy nose of a hard drinker, slumped for most of the day on the same bar stool that he always had to sit on and usually spouted a totally negative view on all aspects of life. The locals had laughed at him behind his back and called him a local character, for which read, miserable old sod. They had occasionally bought him drinks. God knows why. It was a matter of astonishment to those not in the know that The Barfly was married and they pitied his wife. Still, Price wasn't as bad as The Barfly and Sam thought he might know something of Juno's history, since he was always going on about how he had lived in Sheriford all his life.

Sam was bent over the mower, clearing a wad of damp grass from the blade when a voice sounded almost above him. Jack Price was looking at Sam from over the hedge. A wide, toothy grin across his weather-beaten face.

'Surprise 'ee did I? Ha Ha.' His rumbling laughter rolled into a wheezing cough. Price grinned and spat something back into the road. 'You've got the settin' too low. Wants to cut it high. Leaves mine high to keep the weeds down. At least that's the theory.'

Sam grinned as he finished cleaning the mower and then raised the blade height.

'Thanks, Jack. Oh, don't suppose you saw a woman come out of the churchyard last couple of days? Tall, blonde, yellow print dress? She came in day before yesterday looking for Alec and had no idea that he'd died. Said her name was Juno Randall.'

'Randall eh? There's some of that name down at that big house down the road. Burton House. That's it.'

'Know anything about her?'

'Not much. Her and her husband, he's some sort of City bloke, moved here getting on for two year ago. He drives a red sports car, don't know what sort it is, but 'ee goes too fast for the roads round here. Likely to cause an accident sooner or later. Don't see 'em about much. Have you seen that cat of mine? Damn thing didn't come in last night.'

'Saw him this morning, Jack,' Sam replied innocently.

'Don't feed 'im mind. He's a good ratter and it don't pay to feed 'im too much, case 'ee loses 'is edge. Anyway, can't stop here talkin' all day. I'd better get a paper before they's all gone. Not that there's anything worth readin'. Bloody country's gone to the dogs.' Jack Price carried on grumbling as he walked off down the road, while Sam supressed a grin.

3

S unny day followed sunny day. Sam continued to sift through Alec's possessions. There were innumerable keys of all shapes and sizes. Old bills and receipts from firms that had ceased trading years ago and many letters from family members, going back years. Newspaper cuttings concerning events that had interested Alec at the time but that were now largely forgotten. Wardrobes filled with old clothes that smelled of mothballs. Old radios that didn't work, an old brass shell casing from the First World War, filled with walking sticks. Faded pictures of landscapes and buildings that Sam couldn't identify, oddments of china plates and cups, piles of old bed linen, yellowing with age. Then there were the photograph albums, some of which Sam thought must have been bequeathed to Alec by his family members, long since deceased. Sam studied the men and women dressed in their Sunday best, staring sternly at the camera, posed formally with hands on mock pillars or next to potted plants in the photographer's studio. He had no idea who these people were, although they must ultimately have been some relation to Sam.

Alec's sister-in-law, Sam's mother, had taken Sam as a child to meet 'old Uncle Alec' a couple of times, although he probably wasn't really that old then. Sam's mother had lived far away and so visits seemed to be far and few between, although he remembered that she had always spoken fondly of Alec. Alec had never forgotten Sam's birthday and he was always excited to find a crisp bank note in his birthday card to buy something nice with. Sam looked about him, how on earth was he supposed to sort all this stuff out? There was only him left now; no one for him to lean on for advice. Sam had been surprised to learn that Alec had left Glebe Cottage to him. He had assumed it would have gone to his mother, since Alec had no other living relations. But his mother had died a while before Alec and Sam thought that Alec must have changed his Will accordingly. He gave a sigh and left off sorting to gaze out of the window and try to catch a sight of the chimneys on Burton House.

Sam suddenly felt guilty about poking about in Alec's things. He knew that at some point all the bits and pieces would have to be sorted. Some burned at the end of the garden or thrown away. What was any good could be taken to a local charity shop. All of these things represented Alec's life gradually passing away to nothing. It didn't seem right. Who would know of Alec when all the things had gone, but what else was Sam supposed to do? He looked out of the window, this time at Norton Bowl, the great expanse of grassland that rose up towards Anwin Hill. Alec had said that Norton Bowl was chalky ground. Well drained and good for crops. The air in the room seemed cool and smelled a little musty. Sam needed to get outside and into the fresh air and sunlight. He slammed the back door shut behind him, crossed the lawn and strode through a gap in the hedge that gave onto the field behind. Sam breathed in deeply as he walked and felt in a better mood. Alec had shown him on an old map that a Roman road had once run all the way from Salisbury along the rim of the valley and then down from Anwin Hill. The road had skirted Norton Bowl and then run parallel for a while to the gently flowing Wylye river. Sam wondered if he would find any trace of the old road on the ground. He also wondered whether he might catch sight of Juno, but no one was in sight.

The sun was going down, flooding the valley with a golden light. Sam felt better for his hike up to Anwin Hill and returned to pottering about in the garden in a more positive frame of mind when he heard the throaty sound of a powerful engine in the road. He looked over the hedge and saw the red sports car grind to a sudden stop. A passenger, a woman wearing a long black evening dress got out. Sam could see it was Juno, looking made-up for a formal event.

The driver, also wearing evening dress, jumped out from his side and came round to where she was standing. Sam assumed that he was Juno's husband. A stockily built man of medium height, clean shaven, with a heavy jaw and combed back dark hair that straggled untidily round his neck. A heated conversation developed between them, although Sam couldn't clearly make out what was being said, but the gist of it was that Juno had to come to the event and that she couldn't let him down again. Juno stood, looking defiant, while the man jabbed his finger towards her to emphasise his angry words. Moments later he gripped Juno's arm and forced her back towards the car. Grabbing her hair, he pushed her head down with his free hand and thrust her back into the passenger seat. Sam moved towards the garden gate, ready to intervene but as he did so, the driver ran round the car, jumped in and sped off in a cloud of dust and gravel. As it passed by, Sam saw a flash of a distinctly unhappy looking Juno staring ahead.

Two days later gave Sam the opportunity to call in at Burton House. He hadn't wanted to just charge up to the house to ensure that Juno was okay after the altercation in the road. His appearance might well make things worse, but he didn't feel happy with doing nothing. It was fortunate that an excuse to visit presented itself. A courier had earlier dropped a package off, asking if Sam would take in a parcel for the people at Burton House. The item had needed signing for and no one had answered the door. Sam duly signed, saying he would drop it in later, leaving a relieved driver to continue on his way with his busy schedule.

The gravel crunched under Sam's shoes as he walked up the drive to Burton House. He could see the extent of the building clearly and made for the front door. Sam was thinking of Juno when a voice barked out nearby. He stopped in surprise and looked round and saw a man emerge from a gate in a low wall running from the side of the house.

'What do you want?' It was the driver of the red sports car. The man scowled as he strode towards Sam. 'Well, what is it?'

'Um, courier left this with me as he couldn't get a reply earlier.' Sam held out the parcel. 'I live up the road and said I'd drop it in to you.'

The man grunted in acknowledgement. 'Well, I was here. He couldn't have tried very hard.' The frown didn't leave his face, which was flushed. He held out a pudgy hand, with thick, manicured fingers for the parcel, which Sam handed to him. The man nodded and then turned away and made for the side gate without any further word. There was nothing Sam could meaningfully achieve so he turned around and returned to Glebe Cottage, feeling a little deflated.

4

It was another bright day outside, but ten in the morning found
Sam inside Glebe Cottage in a dark living room and in a restless
mood. He didn't know what to do next and any suggestions he
made to himself he then discarded. He had sorted out the majority
of Alec's correspondence and papers, much of which Sam had stuffed
into black bin bags for burning at the end of the garden. Some old
photographs of long-gone relations Sam had kept aside. People
sitting stiffly for their studio portraits looked as if they belonged to a
different world. Yet, they were his relations and in the vast scheme of
things the times that they lived in, the 1920s, 1930s, etc., were not
that far removed from his own, certainly less than one hundred years
and just about within a person's lifetime. It was the formal clothes
and the haircuts that seemed to make them look so much older than
they probably were. That and the stern looks on the faces as they
tried not to move for the camera. Fortunately, Alec had written on
the backs of some of the photos who the people were. Sam was well
through the clearing of the cottage so he must soon decide what to
do with the place. He remembered Juno asking if he was going to
live there. Sam supposed that he could. He had no ties now. His
long-term girlfriend, Ellie, had suddenly announced that life with
Sam wasn't working for her. That she needed to spread her wings and
reach her potential. Whatever that was, Sam thought bitterly. He
had found out soon after that Ellie had simply gone off with Gavin
Roberts, a good-looking rugby player and well-heeled insurance
agent with a big modern house and was now on his own after he had
dumped his previous girlfriend. Hot on the heels of that upsetting
upheaval, Sam had been made redundant from the law firm where
he worked in property sales. The work was dull and dry and to Sam

it seemed that property and money appeared to bring out the worst in some people. Still, the work had paid the bills, which was all he could ask for. It had provided for his life with Ellie. They had a nice, rented house and most of the good things that society deemed to be prizes worth striving for in an effort to acquire and maintain status. Sam had known that Ellie had sometimes chafed against the fact that they couldn't go out and about more often, but he had thought they were happy together. How could he have not seen it coming? Ellie had taken to going to the gym and enjoyed it. Enjoyed meeting Gavin Roberts as it turned out. Sam had actually been pleased that Ellie was doing something she enjoyed and meeting people, while he preferred to spend time sketching and painting. Not that he thought he was any good at it, although several people had been kind enough to say that he showed real talent. Yeah, Sam had thought, but not good enough to pay the rent on his 'nice house' now that he had lost his job and Ellie had gone. Perhaps moving into Alec's cottage might not be too bad a move. A fresh start, a bit of breathing space and then search for another job. Maybe a change in career? Then an image flashed into Sam's mind. Juno wrapped around by golden sunlight. Sam wished he could paint her, keep that moment forever fresh. Juno, Juno, her name sounded in his head like a chant. Wasn't it the name of the Roman Queen of the Gods? Sam shook himself and reached for a plastic bag to fill with rubbish. 'For Christ's sake,' he muttered to himself. 'Get a fucking grip. She's married, lives in a whacking great house, is probably loaded and is not going to be interested in you. She's a bit odd, probably a nutter.' Sam dismissed Juno from his mind and clutching a bag of paper strode briskly from the cottage in the direction of the bonfire site at the end of the garden.

Beyond the garden hedge, Alec had also owned a small, oblong shaped field, bordered by tall, thick hedges that he had apparently been reluctant to keep trimmed down. At the end of the field, the ground dipped down into a small amphitheatre, set about by great old oak trees that kept the site in deep shadow for most of the time. In the centre of the ring of trees stood a small dolmen. Three large upright stones, topped by a great grey slab, all pickled with moss and lichen. The uprights were sited close together and what with the shadow afforded by the trees, the inside of the dolmen was quite dark. Sam had remembered visiting the strange place as a small child. He had wandered out of the garden and across the field, attracted by the tall, dark trees. The adults had been scared when they found that Sam had left the garden, although nothing had happened to him and no one had shouted at him for wandering away. Though there had been a lot of tension in the air. Uncle Alec had been very kind and had simply said that a small boy could easily fall into a hole in the ground, which would be terrible for Sam because if he couldn't be found then he might miss tea. Not long after, Sam's mother had moved away for work and due to the distance involved visits to Uncle Alec became more infrequent. Apparently after Sam's incident, Uncle Alec had installed a gate made of iron bars that effectively blocked any entrance into the dolmen. Sam had all but forgotten about his childhood escapade over the years and the sight of the rusty iron gate securing the dolmen had come as something of a surprise when he'd walked out to see the field a couple of weeks ago.

Sam had no idea what would happen when he eventually managed to force open the gate. Stepping through into the dark interior of the dolmen Sam couldn't see clearly and moved slowly forward, with hands outstretched. He felt a dense, prickly object that had a sort of coconut smell. It was possible to move slowly forward and then, suddenly, the sparse grass of the dolmen floor gave way into a narrow, earthy path that stretched ahead between two tall sandy banks on either side, topped with tufts of Marram grass. Sunlight filtered through the plants and Sam was aware of a salty tang in the air, which felt odd. The path soon opened into a great expanse of heaped sand dunes, dotted thickly with clumps of Marram. Sam felt his jaw drop as he took in the sight of the dunes, the sunlight sparkled on a limitless expanse of sea water. He closed his eyes and then opened them again. The water was still there. He walked slowly forward and looked about. Just an endless vista of grassy dunes and sea. There was no other living soul in sight. Sam wondered if he might be experiencing the onset of some mental trouble and bent down to touch the sand. It felt like what he assumed was normal sand. He picked up a handful and stared at the grains as they ran through his fingers. This really was ridiculous he told himself and then a thought came to him. Had Uncle Alec known about this place? After all, why was the gate there and why had they all been so anxious when Sam, as a child, had wandered towards the dolmen? Sam suddenly felt afraid. This was too unreal, there was no logic to it. He turned and ran back along the path and was mightily relieved to find himself in the dark interior of the dolmen. He went out through the gate and with a screech of rusty hinges slammed it shut behind him. Everything in front of him was exactly as it had been moments before. If this was some sort of mental aberration, how could reality appear before him again, without any form of distortion or upset? Sam ran back across the field to the cottage and made a cup of tea and put some washing on. He stood watching the machine go through its cycles from wash, rinse, spin. All things he took for granted and yet, when he considered it, someone had to have designed all of this. Sam convinced himself that by thinking this way he must be normal so what he had just experienced was perhaps normal as well. Well, not normal in that sense, how could it be? Go through a gate in the depths of the English countryside and emerge into a seaside. That sort of thing could only happen in sci fi.

Ever since the discovery, as Sam called it, of what he thought was an alternative reality, he became watchful and observant of ordinary everyday things going on round the cottage, as if trying to catch out an abnormality and thus prove to himself that at least one of the realities was in his mind. Nothing seemed to indicate that anything was wrong, so a few days later Sam returned to the dolmen, this time somewhat furtively as he didn't wish to attract any attention and he carried with him a large, heavy stick. Sam pushed his way through the dolmen and ended up again at the same place as before. He was intrigued to see his footprints, as he had made them on his first visit. Despite his fears, the place appeared to be the same as he had left it. Again, there was no sign of life about and this time Sam felt emboldened to walk cautiously forward out of the dunes and towards the beach. Carefully scanning all around him, he trod on the damp sand and studied his footsteps as he made them. If this was some form of illusion, then whoever was doing it was bloody good and for what reason? What could be the purpose of putting Sam into some false reality?

He poked his stick into the water as the wave crept gently forward and divided round the stick. It didn't vanish, or catch fire and Sam slowly gave the wet end of the stick the lightest of touch. It was damp and smelled of sea water. He stood for a long time gazing out upon the flat horizon and at one point was excited to think that he may have seen birds, that looked like gulls of some sort, flying high overhead. Then the sun seemed to dip towards the western horizon and Sam thought that something like the golden rays that streamed across the blue sky couldn't be faked. Neither could the warmth on his body from the great golden globe out over the sea. It must be real. The problem was, who to tell? Someone to unburden his new knowledge to. To share this incredible find with. Sadly, there was no one in his life that Sam could tell of this wonder.

At one point he had toyed with the idea of telling Juno what lay beyond the dolmen and had immediately squashed the idea. How do you tell someone that you had apparently found a way into another dimension, place, existence, call it what you will? No, that was best kept to himself. Besides, he knew nothing about Juno, just beyond what he could see of her and that was enough to make him lose his senses if he wasn't careful. Anyway, enough. Juno obviously had a husband and a comfortable lifestyle. She wouldn't want anything to do with him. Then there was the thought in Sam's mind that Juno looked as if she had troubles of her own and probably couldn't deal with him unloading some preposterous revelations of another world upon her. So that was it, keep silent. Sam went to the dolmen and the seaside beyond, as he now called it, a couple more times. On one occasion he had taken a deckchair and a bottle of lemonade and sat at ease under the foreign sun, eyes closed as he faced out to sea and tried to cease thinking.

5

For once, it seemed, the blue summer sky was not in evidence. Cloud had descended, the air was muggy and it felt that rain was not far away. Good for the gardens as Jack Price had muttered over the hedge earlier that morning. Sam walked the short distance to the Sheriford village stores. He almost bumped into a stocky man at the entrance to the shop, with his dark hair swept back from his face and Sam suddenly realised that it was the man who had he had given the parcel to, the man who had argued with Juno outside the red sports car. Must be the husband. Like the last time Sam had met him, he seemed to be scowling and his face was flushed red, whether by exercise, or sheer ill humour it wasn't clear. Immediately behind him, Sam noticed Juno, wearing a dark blue sweatshirt and jeans and large sunglasses that covered a lot of her face. Sam instinctively smiled and said hello. The smile and greeting seemed to fluster Juno and she forced a tight smile. The man turned his head towards her and raised his eyebrows enquiringly.

'Oh Nathan, this is Mr Darking. He lives up at Glebe Cottage,' said Juno casually.

The man swung his attention back to Sam and a glint of recognition flashed across his face.

'Oh, yes, you dropped a parcel in. So, you're at the cottage. Been there long?'

'Couple of months or so, just sorting the place out. It was my Uncle Alec's house.'

The man looked over Sam's shoulder, his pale grey eyes already focussing elsewhere.

'Better be going, Juno,' he said and brushed past Sam and out of the shop. Juno followed, her head held low, intent on not meeting Sam's smile.

Sam selected a newspaper and picked up a bottle of milk from the chilled cabinet and took them to the checkout. Little Mr Ferris, the shopkeeper, gave a brief smile as Sam handed over a bank note.

'Oh, Mr Ferris, could I also have a book of first class stamps please?'

Mr Ferris nodded and drew out a pack from a drawer in the counter.

'They've gone up again,' he said apologetically. 'I suppose it's down to people doing everything online nowadays. Not many send letters now, even cards. Seem to sell fewer of them too.'

'Well, I like to defy social trends,' said Sam. If I had anyone to send cards to, he thought.

'By the way, the couple just in here, are they local?' Sam asked innocently, trying to draw more than Jack Price had told him. 'I think I've seen them before, or at least him.'

'Mr and Mrs Randall,' said Mr Ferris, closing his till. 'They live at Burton House, big place, not far down from you but on the other side of the road. She's very pleasant, but he, well, shall we say, he's not someone I could get on with. Rude, I'd say. My missus saw him out in the road last week and she said, "good morning", like you do and he totally ignored her, looking down his beaky nose, she said.'

'Well, I suppose it takes all sorts,' said Sam diplomatically.

'Drives that flash car of his like a maniac. He'll hit someone one of these days … Good morning, Marjorie. How are you?' An older lady had entered the shop.

'Morning, Bert,' she said. 'Good morning, Mr Darking.'

'Hello, Mrs Landon, trust you're well. Please, it's Sam. I haven't been called Mr Darking since I had to go to the headmaster at school for breaking a window.'

'Sam it is.' The woman smiled. 'Marjorie to you from now on. Looks like rain later.'

'Yes,' said Sam. 'But good for the gardens, as Jack Price told me.'

'Jack okay?' Marjorie asked. 'Haven't seen him for a while. He did collar me a couple of weeks ago and I had to hear all about his problem with his legs. Took me ages to escape. I think he's lonely, but there's only so much you can listen to about other people's ill health before it becomes depressing.'

Sam continued with a little banter with Marjorie and Bert Ferris before he took his leave. He had managed not to think about Juno for a couple of days, but as he walked slowly past Burton House on his way home, he wondered about her. He was sure there was something amiss, but he made a point of staring ahead and not looking towards the house.

6

Next morning, just after nine-thirty, Sam saw from an upstairs window at the cottage, the now familiar red sports car zoom off up the road, driven by the man he now knew as Nathan Randall. Some sort of City bloke, Jack Price had said. Was he off to catch a train to London? Bit late if he was. That left Juno on her own in that big house and he wondered if he might call in. Sod that, thought Sam, too complicated. The day was overcast but warm and he felt in need of some exercise. He went downstairs, looked out his walking boots and planned a brisk trek across Norton Bowl and up to Anwin Hill. You could see for miles up there, all the villages and farms spread out below like toys.

The walk had done him good. He'd had to puff a bit to climb the steep green banks of Anwin Hill and had enjoyed the effort. It was always windy up on Anwin. Blows the cobwebs off being up there he'd thought and had taken binoculars to see distant points of interest more clearly. Almost without thinking, Sam found himself adjusting the lenses to get a clear view of Burton House. Juno wasn't in sight and Sam felt annoyed with himself that he'd ended up checking the place out. He put the binoculars back in their case and tramped down the hill, keeping an eye on a bank of dark cloud that was building from the south-west. As Sam skirted a field hedge, walking in the direction of the cottage, it began to drizzle. He had on an old shooting jacket of Alec's that had fitted and he didn't mind the cooling drops that fell on his face. He picked up his speed, swishing through the long grass of the field headland. The hedges were green and the fields looked in good condition. Sam felt in good spirits as he climbed over a field gate and headed for the back entrance to Glebe Cottage. He sniffed the smell of rain and glanced over towards St

Michael's. Dark clouds now framed the church tower and they were moving across the valley at speed. Just as Sam unlocked the back door and went inside it began to tip down. Hanging up his coat on a peg on the back of the door Sam was glad that he hadn't been caught outside. With the heavy cloud passing low overhead, the house had become dark, so he turned on the standard lamp in the sitting room. The rain was beating down on the roof and gurgling down the gutters and pipes when Sam glanced out of a window and was surprised to see Juno standing in the church porch. As he watched, she stepped forward and ran into the road and then stood, looking at Glebe Cottage. What on earth are you doing? Sam thought, as he stared at her, standing in the road, being soaked. He grabbed the jacket that he had just worn and ran out into the rain.

'Juno,' Sam shouted. 'Come on in, you'll be soaked.' She just looked at him but didn't move. Sam came up to her and threw his coat over her shoulders. 'Come on in.' Juno looked vacantly up and down the road, the rain hammering down on the dark tarmac and flowing down the ditches and then seemed to come to. Sam grabbed her hand and urged her into the open cottage door.

'Christ, Juno, you're soaked through,' said Sam. 'What on earth were …' He stopped speaking as he saw the anxious, frightened look on Juno's face, her golden hair plastered over her forehead and down the sides of her wet face. Her eyes were wide open and Sam felt afraid for her. Something must be wrong.

'I didn't know what else to do,' Juno stammered. 'I had wanted … then it looked like rain. I thought you were out and was going to leave it. Then, when it started, I went into the church porch. I saw the light come on and knew you were back.' The words babbled out.

'Juno,' said Sam gently. 'You're soaked through. Just sit down a minute and I'll find you some towels and dry clothes. We'll get you dry before we say anything else, okay?' Juno simply nodded and slumped down near the old stone fireplace. Sam threw some sticks and bits of wood on top of a fire lighter and soon had a small fire going.

'It's a bit dark and cold in here but this will burn up brighter soon. Keep an eye on it would you? I'll be back in a minute.'

Juno sat still, staring at the flames as they flickered and spread round the sticks. Sam raced upstairs and after a furious rummage in cupboards and drawers gathered up a couple of bath towels, some clothes and a hair dryer.

When he returned to the sitting room, he found Juno kneeling in front of the fire and had obviously added more wood to it.

'Here's some towels. I've brought a big jersey of mine. I know it's far too big for you but it's clean and will keep you warm. There's also a clean pair of my jeans. Nothing else would be any good, I think. Just pull the belt in and roll up the legs and you'll be alright. We'll put your clothes in the tumble dryer and soon get them dry again. Electric socket down by the fireplace if you want to plug the dryer in. I'll leave you for a minute and get a hot drink going. Tea or coffee?'

'Coffee, thanks,' Juno replied. Sam slipped away and headed for the nearby kitchen. As he got out cups and searched for the coffee jar in the units, he glanced at the kitchen door. It had a glass panel in the top half and Sam couldn't help but catch a glimpse of Juno as she pulled off her wet shirt over her head and stood before the fire in a black bra, before towelling herself dry. Sam felt a little embarrassed at the sight of her slender, pale figure and then saw the bruises on her arms and noticed that Juno lightly touched a big bruise on her side. Sam frowned as he made the coffees. He hung back in the kitchen and then looked back through the glass panel in the door. Juno had pulled on his jersey and was rolling up the legs of his jeans that hung loosely on her. She began to dry her hair when Sam decided that he could go back into the sitting room and try to find out what was really happening.

The fire was burning brightly and Juno was sat on the floor, running her fingers through her hair. Sam picked up her jeans and shirt.

'I'll just put these in the dryer.' He went off into the utility room, next to the kitchen and placed Juno's clothes in the dryer and switched it on. The machine rumbled away and Sam picked up two mugs of coffee from the kitchen and went back into the sitting room. He placed one down on the fireplace in front of Juno and held on to the other as he stood nearby. Juno looked up as she tried to tease her hair into shape and smiled.

'Thank you. You're very kind. Sorry to have been a nuisance.'

'You're not a nuisance.' Sam laughed. 'Glad to be able to help. Your clothes are in the dryer, soon be okay. At least Alec had all mod cons.'

'You must miss him,' said Juno, her big blue eyes looking at him, not scared now.

'We weren't close. Mum needed to move away for work when I was young, so we only had occasional visits. Dad, Alec's older brother, died when I was not much more than a baby, but Mum always maintained contact with Alec. I enjoyed coming to see him. He seemed very old then, but of course I doubt that he really was. Kids always seem to see anyone older than themselves as ancient. Mum always spoke highly of Alec, well, you've met him yourself.'

Juno looked blank for a moment.

'You said a while back that Alec was going to let you have a book on local history?' Sam prompted.

'Oh yes, of course. I'd forgotten. I first met Alec in the shop here and then I saw him a couple of times out walking in the village. My husband, Nathan, was working away a lot then and Alec was an entertaining source of local information shall we say.' Juno smiled.

'I think I remember saying that we made toast in front of this fire last November. The power had gone off in the whole of the village at that time. Nathan was away and I went to the shop to see if I could buy a hot water bottle. We're all electric, which is fine until the power goes off. It didn't occur to me how I was going to heat the water to put in the bottle when the power was off! Obviously not thinking straight. I met Alec in the road and as soon as he realised my predicament, he invited me here. It was so nice. He'd made the fire up and it was warm and comfortable and he had candles everywhere, on saucers and in bottles. I love candlelight. It took me back to my childhood.' Juno looked up from her coffee mug. 'Sounds like the rain's eased off. I should be going, don't want to impose.'

'No imposition.' Sam smiled.

'Nathan will be back later and I wanted to cook something special tonight.'

'Lucky guy, I tend to resort to beans on toast and if I'm being adventurous, I might fry an egg as well. I can cook, it's just that it's a faff for one and I hate washing up after. I'll go and see if your clothes are dry.'

Sam kept well away as Juno dressed. She found him in the kitchen and handed him his jeans and jersey, neatly folded.

'Thanks for helping me out. You've been very kind.'

'I'm usually here, if you find yourself getting soaked again.' Sam laughed. 'I know where the garden hose is and can do a good job on you.'

Juno gave Sam a sad sort of smile as she left. He watched her from the window walking slowly back down the road towards her house and she looked so solitary that it made his heart sink.

7

Sam hadn't seen Juno for nearly a week. He'd finally got on top of the overgrown garden and imposed some order upon the unruly plants and grass. Not that he classed himself as a gardener, not being sure of what he was doing. He had gone through the iron gate and had sat on the sun drenched beach for quite a while, but it hadn't given him the relaxation that he'd hoped for. He felt adrift, as if wanting something to happen that would kickstart his life into action. In the meantime, what to do? The cottage was all sorted and in good order and while not having made any final decision, Sam thought it may be increasingly good sense to see how he got on living there. If he lived carefully, he could manage, at least he had no debts to service. Sam thought about engaging the creative mood that he had once enjoyed but had now long neglected. He planned to drive into Salisbury and pick up some paper and paint and perhaps do a little sketching. At least he would be getting out of the village for a while.

Next Saturday morning Sam called in at the village shop.

'Morning, Sam,' called out Bert Ferris as he balanced on a pair of folding steps, putting boxes of tissue and toilet rolls up on a high shelf.

'How're you getting on sorting the cottage out?' Sam was pleased to have gained a form of acceptance by the use of his first name.

'Morning, Bert.' Sam nodded at the stack of toilet rolls. 'You got news of a party taking place hereabouts?'

Bert looked nonplussed for a second and then laughed.

'Ha ha. Well, you never know. We must be able to supply the customer with whatever he needs, whenever. Mind you, if there's a run on them, I might be able to put prices up. Supply and demand, see?'

'Excellent, Bert, very funny.' Sam laughed. 'Actually, I'm thinking of making a curry tonight, so perhaps I'd better have a couple of extra ones. Still, all's well. Must have smoked Jack Price out with all the bonfires I've been having. I think virtually all the rubbish is gone now and I've taken the best stuff to charity shops.'

'I hate to think how long it would take to clear our house out. My missus is such a hoarder.'

'Do it on the quiet, Bert. Bit at a time so she won't notice. You can always come up to mine for a secret bonfire.'

'No good, Sam. She's got eyes like an eagle. Never misses anything.'

Sam grinned and paid for the few groceries he'd selected, then left the shop. His eyes had to adjust from the dark interior to brilliant sunshine outside and he nearly collided with Juno on her way in.

'Hi, Juno, how are you?'

'Sam!' Juno seemed surprised to see him. 'I'm okay.' She was wearing a long sleeved blue cotton shirt and jeans and a floral pattern scarf wrapped around her neck. She had her large sunglasses on.

'Hottest day of the year I heard on the radio,' said Sam by way of conversation.

'Yes, I heard that too,' Juno replied.

'Fancy a coffee later?' Sam asked casually.

Juno shook her head. 'Thanks, nice idea, but I've a lot on at the moment. Nathan is off to Qatar later today and I've just come out to get him some toothpaste to take.'

'Qatar eh? Probably as hot here as it is out there. Anyway, nice to see you.' Sam walked on up the road, leaving Juno to enter the shop, while he thought about her reserved manner.

About three, Sam was sat out in the garden in an old deckchair that he had found in Alec's glory hole under the stairs. He'd also found a large, faded green umbrella and had tied it to a post that supported the clothesline. It was almost too hot to move and Sam drained his glass of elderflower cordial and thought about getting another, the trouble was that it would require the effort of getting up out of the chair. Then he heard the front gate click. He glanced up and saw Juno walk up the path. She'd changed into a long, white cotton dress, again with long sleeves and was wearing the same floral pattern scarf round her neck. Sam stood up and smiled.

'Glad to see you came. Nathan gone, then?'

Juno nodded. 'I drove him to the station to catch the three-thirty. He'll be back on Wednesday and I'll go and pick him up.'

Sam indicated his deckchair. 'Come and sit in the shade. I'll get another chair. Would you like a drink? It's elderflower or elderflower I'm afraid. Didn't think to get anything else in.'

Juno eased herself into the deckchair that Sam had vacated under the shade of the umbrella.

'Ah, this is nice. I find this heat quite draining, but I don't want to sit indoors.'

'I know what you mean,' said Sam as he handed Juno a tall glass of elderflower cordial. He then returned to the cottage and emerged a few moments later with another old deckchair, which he plonked down next to Juno.

'I've got to be a bit careful.' Sam laughed as he lowered himself slowly onto the mottled canvas. 'It's a bit past it and I don't want to go through it when I sit down. Looks like it might have come off the Titanic.'

Juno smiled and took a long drink from her glass and looked out over the garden towards Anwin Hill. They sat in companionable silence for a while and then Sam said, 'How are you then, Juno?'

Juno turned to face him with a surprised look on her face.

'Fine, why do you ask?'

'You don't seem fine. I know it's none of my business, but you don't sound okay and you don't look it. Can I help, or at least listen?'

Juno scowled. 'Don't be ridiculous. There's nothing wrong with me. Absolutely nothing. What on earth made you think there was?'

Hauling herself up out of her chair, Juno wordlessly handed Sam her glass and walked towards the garden gate. Sam said nothing but felt sad to see her go and inwardly cursed himself for having overstepped the mark. Then, at the gate, Juno stopped and half turned.

'Do others in the village think there's something wrong with me, or is it just you?'

Sam stood up and moved a short way towards Juno.

'Well, for what it's worth, Bert Ferris thinks you're very pleasant.'

'Pleasant?' Juno scoffed. 'What an ordinary word, damned with faint praise.' Juno thought for a moment and looked up at the cloudless blue sky, then sighed.

'It's my birthday tomorrow. Don't know why I said that. Not a pleasant thing, though.'

'If you're on your own why not come over for coffee tomorrow,' said Sam

'Why?' Juno asked tartly. 'Are you going to feel sorry for me since I'm obviously not, in your eyes, at all well?'

'Not at all. I know nothing about you and have no agenda. It's just that if it's your birthday you should be able to enjoy it. No fuss of course.'

Juno looked at Sam for a moment, but he couldn't read her expression through her sunglasses.

'Okay, then.' It sounded like a reluctant concession and then she was gone.

8

Late evening the following day found Sam sat in the rear garden, eyes closed and a straw hat that he'd found in the attic slumped over his forehead. His mobile was on his lap, playing some of his library of downloaded records.

'That's nice, what is it?'

Sam jumped and pushed the hat back off his face.

'Oh, I didn't think you'd come. Happy Birthday by the way.'

Juno stood at the side of the cottage, still wearing her large sunglasses.

'It's Goldfrapp, track called *Fly Me Away*,' said Sam. 'Come and sit down,' and he indicated the other deckchair that he'd left out from yesterday. Juno smiled and sat down, spreading her long, floaty black dress over her legs. The track changed.

'That sounds good too. Breathless and dreamy.'

'Goldfrapp again,' said Sam. '*Time Out from the World.*'

'Like it,' said Juno as she settled back in the chair. 'Good title. I could do with some of that.'

'What? Time away from everything?' Sam smiled. 'I think we all need that every so often. Look, as it's your birthday, I did go into Salisbury this morning and get a couple of things.'

Juno raised an eyebrow.

'I hope you haven't gone to any trouble. You did say no fuss. I'm not really in a party mood.'

'No.' Sam grinned. 'I didn't think Bert Ferris would have what I was after and I didn't want him asking the inevitable, like are you having a party? For which I would have to lie. Something like the parrot's died and I'm having a wake. Then Bert would be all serious and say, "I didn't know you had a parrot" and so it goes on. Start with

34

a lie and it's best to keep it simple and remember what you say. Mind you, if I had clammed up it would have spurred him on to make enquiries of Marjorie Landon and it would have got completely out of hand.'

Juno laughed and took off her sunglasses.

'It could have been a Norwegian Blue, the parrot.'

'Excellent! A Monty Python fan. I wouldn't have put you down as one. Bit far back now,' said Sam.

'Quality survives. Dad loved it and had the complete DVD collection, which he often played when I was at home. It's so bizarre and funny. It's a shame there's nothing as good on the TV now.'

Sam nodded in agreement.

'Fancy that, a fellow Python fan. The day is definitely looking up. When I said I'd been to Salisbury, I did get some provisions for this moment. Well, I hoped you might come over. Anyway, stay here and I'll bring them out.'

Sam got up from his deckchair, trying to avoid looking at Juno's black eye, visible now that she had taken her sunglasses off.

'Sorry I was moody yesterday,' Juno said. 'Bad day.'

'No problem. Glad you've come.' Sam went off inside the cottage and re-emerged with a small picnic table and some paper plates.

'See. No expense spared. Now for the main event.' Sam smiled as he went back inside and came out bearing a wooden tray and holding in one hand a bottle. Sam set the tray down on the table.

'There, a not-the-birthday-cake,' he announced, waving a hand towards the Colin the Caterpillar cake that took pride of place on an old blue china plate, together with a bowl of crisps and two glass tumblers.

'Brilliant.' Juno laughed as Sam cut a couple of pieces of cake and filled the glasses from a Chardonnay bottle.

Later, when the cake was nearly half gone and little wine left in the bottle, Juno turned to Sam.

'Thanks for this. It was very kind of you and for not asking about the black eye. Just as well it's summer, I can wear sunglasses, but at night, it's a bit ridiculous.'

'I've heard that arnica might be helpful, to relieve the bruising,' said Sam casually. Juno drained her glass and then held it out with a smile for Sam to refill. He emptied the bottle into her glass and grinned.

'Not to worry, I have another in the kitchen.' He got up and soon returned with another bottle and topped up Juno's glass.

'You know, it's odd,' said Juno. 'Here I am drinking wine in the garden of a stranger's house. It's my thirty-fourth birthday and I did feel wretched, but not now. This has been the nicest time I've had for ages …' Juno sniffed and looked away towards Anwin Hill, standing firm against the darkening sky.

Sam leaned forward and gently touched Juno's shoulder.

'Strange maybe, but a stranger I would hope not. If you need a friend, as I said, I have no agenda.'

'Why are you being so kind to me?' Juno asked, and Sam saw a tear roll down her face and felt sad for her.

'You look adrift and unloved,' said Sam briefly, as he topped up his glass. 'The first time I saw you in the churchyard I thought you were utterly beautiful and yet unhappy.'

Juno snorted. 'Being so-called beautiful doesn't stop you being unhappy, believe me. We all must pay for our mistakes. You're a good person but why are you here alone?' Juno downed the contents of her glass and breathed out deeply.

'Been dumped by my long-term girlfriend. I thought we were happy but she was off at the gym with Gavin Roberts. Didn't see it of course. I was actually pleased that she was having something of an independent social life, that it would be good for us. Then comes poster boy Gavin, big muscles, perfect white teeth and well paid job. Bastard. Then of course I was made redundant. It's only because of

Alec's kindness that I have a roof over my head. I wish he was still here, but wishes are pointless.'

'Gavin the wanker,' said Juno, a little slurred and then burst out laughing. 'Gavin is a wanker. Gavin is a wanker,' she chanted. 'Oh dear. I've had too much. It always goes to my head. I shouldn't speak like that. What's that saying?' Juno burst out laughing again.

'I think you might mean, in vino veritas,' said Sam. 'We can sometimes tell the truth under the effects of the booze.'

Juno nodded and tried to look serious and then sniggered, before trying to pull herself together.

'Do you miss her, your girlfriend?'

'I did. I suppose the best way I can describe losing the loving feeling is like a ruptured fuel line. It spews out all over the place when the pipe is cut and the feeling is lost and then it eventually dries up and, as they say, life goes on. It has to, you have no choice about that, but the memories remain and keep roaming around in your head, but finally, the time spent confronting those memories becomes more spaced out.'

'I was happy, once,' said Juno. 'Normal family unit as they say. Mum and Dad and a sister, Angela. We lived in a very nice house in Suffolk. Dad was a senior partner in a financial investment firm. Mum did the homemaking thing, making sure that all functioned seamlessly and enjoyed lunching with friends and doing charity works. All very dull and middle class I suppose. I did quite well at school. A good average I was often called and eventually went to uni without knowing why or even wanting to particularly. It just seemed a soft option, putting things off. I got a history degree and after that drifted for a bit, not knowing what to do. Of course, Dad was well off and made it easy for me to drift. Anyway, I got a job with the County Council's archive section and really enjoyed it. Then I met Nathan. He was the son of a business buddy of Dad's. He's older than me by about ten years. Nathan that is.' Juno laughed loudly. 'We met at a party and seemed to click. He was very attentive and charming. That's one thing he is good at. Charming those who can be of use to him. He didn't go on and on about football or cars, which bores me silly. Dad was very pleased and so was Mum when Nathan proposed. I accepted and from then on was caught up in the wedding nonsense. It seemed to have a life of its own and I began to feel that I couldn't buck it. I didn't want to let people down and after all, it wouldn't be so bad. So much was going on to make this the perfect fairy tale wedding that I felt that I couldn't say, no, hang on, can I think about this please?'

'So, you weren't convinced you were doing the right thing?' Sam said quietly.

'A nagging thought did intrude every so often. I sometimes felt that it must be a natural case of nerves and that I was being foolish over leaving the security of home, all that I was familiar with. Angela was the only one I could really talk to about it. She's a bit younger than me and she said that if I was not absolutely certain, then I should not go through with it. Like the guy in *Four Weddings and a Funeral*. But the thought of letting everyone down! On the day, I managed to conceal my worries and it all passed in a blur of colour and people talking at me. I was the centre of attention. Brides are supposed to love it, but I didn't.'

'What made you uncertain?' Sam asked.

'Nathan was very capable, but it seemed that the longer we were together, the more controlling he became. I suppose on reflection it must have always been a part of his character. I didn't see it at first. Then it was, wear this, don't wear that. Why are you seeing so and so, where are you going and when will you be back? You shouldn't go there. That sort of thing. I managed to put up with it for a while, until I realised that I had virtually lost contact with old friends and only socialised with Nathan and people he knew from his work. He was in his Dad's firm and doing very well and very fast. We wanted for nothing in the material sense. In the meantime, I managed to keep working, although Nathan was not at all happy about it. He kept running the job down and said he was earning more than enough to keep the both of us in the manner to which he wanted.

'His mother never worked and although mine didn't either, she was an independent person and Dad's view was that she would always bring something home to talk about from all her activities.'

'You didn't end up in baby land, then?'

'No, thank goodness,' said Juno, frowning. 'It never seemed to happen. Nathan became increasingly frustrated at the thought that I couldn't produce a son and heir for him. It started to go wrong very quickly. Then I was made redundant due to Council cutbacks, which obviously pleased Nathan. There was nothing comparable about that I could apply for. I even thought of applying for a job in the local library, but Nathan vetoed that as being beneath me. Probably couldn't stand the idea of someone he knew seeing me working in a library. Got very stroppy about it all. Then again, I didn't have much time to deal with that problem before a real bombshell erupted in our midst. Mum went off with one of Dad's work friends. I had no idea; she never mentioned or gave any hint that she was unhappy with Dad. He was totally wiped out by it all and became very bitter about it. Mum and her so-called friend went to live in Spain, out of the way of it all I suppose. It was actually very sad, after having been out there for a couple of months, she was killed in a boating accident. Dad became quite withdrawn after that. I think he still cared for her and had some notion that she might come back to him. Angela was still at home then, but she went to uni and so he was left alone. I was really worried about him, but surprisingly, he met a woman, a friend of one of his clients and she seemed to break the dark spell and made him happy again. That was a few years ago. He sold out of the business and he and Mac became an item.'

'Mac, that's an odd name,' said Sam, crunching one of the last crisps.

'Short for McKenna. Apparently, it's a family name. McKenna Arthurson. Anyway, they now live in the States. Angela got married three years ago and lives in New Zealand, where she's happily married to a film director. So, that's my family history. Christ, I've never talked so much in one go. What about your family history?'

'Since we're being open,' said Sam, 'I can tell you that I am very boring. My dear mother died unexpectedly five years ago and I lost my job in a law firm, which didn't exactly bother me as I never liked it. One of those things that you drift into, but never seem to be able to get out of. I think it was simply a way of paying the bills. Couldn't keep my girlfriend Ellie from going off with Mr Universe Gavin Roberts though.'

'Gavin the wanker,' Juno interrupted with a laugh. 'That's how we'll refer to him from now on.'

'Good idea.' Sam grinned. 'Ideally, I'd never have to refer to him again. Then Uncle Alec died, another unexpected death, leaving all this to me. All these unexpected deaths doesn't bode well, does it? I don't need to work again as my needs are very modest, but what I've been fortunate to gain has been at too high a price. There, that's it. I am nothing more than a footnote to be forgotten.'

'Bloody hell, what a depressing outlook,' said Juno. 'From what I see, you're in charge of you own destiny.' She placed her now empty glass on the picnic table. 'I'm into something I can't seem to get out of. Nathan's now very high up in the firm but seems to have a number of clients who don't seem right. Shifty sort of people that might be inclined to resolve problems with hired muscle. Nathan appears to get on with them, which is a bit of a worry. Sometimes he brings them home for dinner and I must play the part of a charming hostess. One or two of them give me the creeps the way they look at me.'

'So, where did the bruises come from?' Sam asked softly. 'Tell me to mind my own business if you like, but it's obvious that you're in trouble and I'd like to be able to help.'

Juno gave a sigh. 'No, it's about time I stopped trying to hide what's going on. It's Nathan. Whatever line of work he's into now exacerbates behaviour that was evident some years ago. The controlling, I can't do anything right. Especially provide him with a son, although that hasn't cropped up in a while, but I know it's not far below the surface. God forbid I fell pregnant with a daughter! One day I accidentally broke an antique vase that had been his grandmother's. He was furious and lashed out with his fist, catching me on the cheek. I was more surprised than hurt and I think he was also surprised at his reaction. He apologised of course and was nice as pie for a couple of days afterwards. Then one day something else happened, I forget what, it was nothing major, but he lost his temper and gripped my arms so tightly that he bruised me and the look on his face, one of real anger, frightened me. Then came the apology again and he put his mood down to immense pressure of work. We ended up moving down here a couple of years ago, to give us a break and change of scenery he said. The place was owned by a friend of Nathan's and in return for some significant help with a financial problem, I never understood what, Nathan got the chance to buy the place at generous terms shall we say. Not that I got any say in the move. I'm more isolated than ever down here.' Juno rose to her feet, a little unsteadily.

'I need a pee then I'd better go. It'll be dark soon.'

'Downstairs, next to the kitchen. You can't miss it,' said Sam. Pity she broke off in full flow he thought. Sam felt he could listen to her gentle voice forever when a wild notion came to mind.

After a while Juno returned. 'It's been lovely. Thank you, Sam, for listening. I do feel better for that.'

'So long as you've had a pleasant time. It was just that, if you wanted, I had something else to show you.'

Juno inclined her head. 'What do you mean, something else?'

'Well, I suppose you could say that I found it here. I think

Alec might have known about it or had some notion and now the knowledge seems to rest with me.'

'Sounds intriguing.' Juno turned to go back inside the cottage.

'No, it's not inside. We have to go up there.' Sam pointed to the end of the garden. 'But first we must take some torches. It's getting dark and we want to see where we're going.'

'What on earth are you talking about, Sam? Needing light? I don't think I can walk very far in these shoes.'

'Stay here, I won't be a moment,' Sam called out over his shoulder as he ran back inside the cottage. He returned with a hurricane lamp hung from a long black metal road with a hook on the end and a hand torch.

'I also brought this,' said Sam, holding up a sweatshirt. 'It's clean, just in case you get cold.'

Sam led the way through the garden and across the adjoining field, with Juno becoming increasingly reluctant, trailing behind.

'Hold on, Sam, is it far? I think I could do with getting back now.'

'Just a moment, we're nearly there,' said Sam excitedly. 'Prepare to be astounded, as I was when I first came here.'

'Okay,' Juno grumbled. 'Just so long as it doesn't take long. Whatever it is we could have come back tomorrow, surely. We could see better then.'

Sam fumbled with the iron gate at the dolmen and applied a light to the lamp. The yellow glow illuminated the stones of the dolmen and the trunks of the surrounding trees.

'Is this it?' Juno sounded distinctly unimpressed. 'Does this lead somewhere?'

'Yes, it does, now follow me closely.' Sam pushed the gate open and went through, followed by Juno.

'Here, have this.' Sam passed the torch back to her. 'Beware of the gorse.'

'Gorse? Where? … Ouch,' said Juno as she stumbled forward.

'Here we are,' said Sam. 'Be amazed.'

Juno flashed the torch light on the ground.

'What the hell is this? It can't be sand, surely?'

'Certainly is. Come on, just a bit further.'

'This is stupid,' Juno snapped. 'There can't be sand here. What's that smell?'

'Sea air, seaweed?' Sam replied. 'Now look at that.'

The huge disc of a silver coloured moon hung over a flat seascape, with small breakers drifting into the shore.

'Bloody hell,' Juno swore, and her mouth gaped open in astonishment. 'This can't be real, Sam, whatever you're doing, stop it. It's not funny. I'm scared now.'

Sam reached for Juno's hand. 'See, touch it's real. The lamp I'm holding shows some of the seashore. Look up at the stars. It's all real. You're not ill or delusional. I'm not pulling any stunt. This is all real. Feel the sand beneath your feet. Can you feel a cool breeze coming in from the sea? Walk with me down to the water's edge and touch the water. It's all real, no joke.'

Juno stood rigidly, looking scared and her eyes flashed wildly about, trying to take everything in all at once. Sam tried to reassure her.

'Look, Juno, you're quite safe. Nothing is going on that can hurt you. To be honest I've wanted to tell you about this before but never thought it right until now.'

Juno put her hands over her eyes and then removed them and stared out to sea.

'Am I going mad?' Juno said to herself. Then she looked at Sam.

'Get me out of here. This cannot be right. This is some invention of my head. Something's very wrong.'

'Okay.' Sam shrugged. 'Come on, follow me and I'll get you back.'

They turned but didn't see two lights come on, a way to the left. Nor did they see a thin white light appear on the seashore. They retraced their steps back to the dolmen and went through the gate and out into the field. Sam and Juno walked back to the cottage in silence and then he had insisted on escorting a now fully sober Juno back to the entrance to her house.

'Sorry,' said Sam. 'I didn't mean to scare you. I thought that if you were feeling so low on your birthday I could show you something marvellous and unexplainable. After all I don't know what's out there, or why, just that it is.'

Juno gave a brief glance at Sam and shook her head then walked on to the front door, leaving Sam to trudge home in the dark feeling small and stupid.

9

Next day promised to be a fine one and Sam decided that a furious bout of gardening and cleaning the cottage might help divert him from his depressed feelings. How on earth, he asked himself again and again, could he have been so idiotic as to drag Juno through the dolmen and into whatever lay beyond on the basis that it was a birthday treat? The lawn had been mown within an inch of its life and the clippings stored in the composter. Sam rubbed sweat from his face and considered that he had done enough and a cold drink was called for. He set up one of the deckchairs, facing the end of the garden and plonked himself down, with a can of beer from the fridge.

Sam was gazing at an odd cloud formation that looked as if it were a ship sailing over Anwin Hill, when he heard footsteps on the gravel path behind the cottage. He twisted round and was very surprised to see Juno come walking towards him. Sam thought she looked a stunner in the small denim shorts that he had seen her wear before, this time with a loose, pale blue shirt, a straw hat and the usual large sunglasses. He leaped up out of the deckchair like a scalded cat, looking sheepishly at Juno.

'I came to say sorry,' said Juno quietly, standing a little awkwardly.

'Sorry?' Sam blurted out. 'You've got nothing to be sorry about. If anything, it's me who is very sorry for having … well … you know, for last night.'

Juno smiled. 'Well. I did think it was going wonderfully until I got a little merry, shall we say, and then you hauled me off to see a huge moon and a seashore. In Sheriford of all places. Lord knows how far we are from the coast. I couldn't believe it. I thought I was having a mental breakdown. To say that I was scared would be an understatement.'

'I should have thought it would make anyone doubt their senses and for that I'm truly sorry,' said Sam. 'In a feeble defence, I really did think it might make you feel, well, happier, I suppose.'

'I did think I was going mad and blamed you for it,' said Juno. 'I went to bed straight after I got home last night. Fell on the bed and woke up this morning and to be truthful, thinking that all I had seen was some form of fantasy or illusion and couldn't think why. The actual reason I came here is when I took my shoes off this morning, I found sand in them and there's nowhere round here that it could have come from. So … that and a sprig of gorse caught in the back of my dress made me think that, maybe, I wasn't dreaming, or inventing the whole weird episode. Anyway, sorry if I was off.'

'Nothing to apologise for,' said Sam firmly. 'Now that you're here and I'm very pleased to see you, can I get you a drink?'

'Yes please. I see you've been busy this morning. The garden's looking good.'

'It's getting there, not that I'm sure I know what I'm doing. I'm just good at cutting things down and digging them up. Have my seat and I'll be back in a minute.'

Sam returned with a long glass of elderflower cordial and ice and another deckchair, which he set up. After a drink, Juno pushed her hat back and looked at Sam.

'Thing is, I was wondering where we did go last night. I can remember things very clearly and I'm now fairly confident I wasn't having a breakdown and that all of this was not a delusion and I was not blind drunk and imagining things.' Juno waved an arm to encompass the garden and the field beyond.

'No, you're not delusional,' said Sam evenly. 'What you think you saw last night, you did. I was there. I saw exactly what you did.'

'Well, if it's an illusion then it's got to be the most original one, for us to see the same thing.' Juno drained her glass and sat back in her chair. 'So, let's start with the idea that what I saw, what we saw last night actually existed. It's beyond belief, save for the evidence of the sand in my shoes.'

'Believe me, it's all real,' said Sam. 'Just don't ask me to explain it, because I can't. I have no idea what it all means, beyond the fact that the place is real.' He paused and looked at Juno.

'It's the same every time, although I've only been once before when it was night.'

'Every time?' Juno gasped and took her sunglasses off. 'You've been there before and you never said?'

'How could I? If I'd said, oh, I've just found a way into an alternative reality at the end of a field and would you like to come and look? You'd have thought I was off my head. It was only because I so wanted something special for your birthday that I made the incredibly stupid decision to take you to see what I knew would be there.' Sam looked embarrassed. 'I did think afterwards that you'd want to steer clear of me and this place if you thought it was weirdo central.'

Juno smiled. 'This is truly strange. I don't think you look like a murderer, or weirdo and believe me nothing like this has ever happened to me before and I want to know more.'

'Okay then. If you want to see the real deal, are you up for coming with me again?'

'Yes, sure. I'd love to know whatever this is.'

'Good. We might as well enjoy our time there, so we're going to need a few things.'

'What sort of things?' Juno looked uncertain.

'Rug to sit on, something cool to drink and suntan lotion.' Sam laughed. 'What did you have in mind? Chainmail, crucifix, bible and holy water?'

'Very funny. No, I have no idea. You've been there before and I trust that you know what you're doing.'

They crossed the field at the end of the garden, keeping to the hedgerow in case, as Sam explained, any nosey so and so caught sight of them and ended up asking questions later.

They soon came to the dolmen and Juno stared up at the trees clustered about that helped shade the place from sunlight.

'Wow, this is amazing. I can imagine kids would love to make camps here and mess about.' Juno stroked one of the dolmen stone uprights. 'This is so old and it seems an unusual place to site one, down here in a dip. You'd think the builders would have placed it on a hilltop, or high ground, to be seen for miles around.'

'How old do you reckon, then?' Sam asked.

'Three to four thousand years, possibly. We touched on them at uni. I think they may have originally been tombs and possibly covered with earth that has eventually worn away to expose the stones. Still, I think the jury's out on what they were for certain. You say this one is on Alec's land?'

'Yes, and you can tell from the gate that he didn't want visitors snooping around.'

'Can't see many knowing about this place anyway. It's a bit remote,' said Juno looking about her.

'I do wonder whether Alec knew what this place was,' said Sam. 'I have a vague childhood memory of coming here when there was no gate. I can recall the adults had been upset by me wandering out here. Alec must have put up the gate later.'

'Do you think there's is any local folklore about people disappearing here? Lost children never found sort of thing,' Juno added dramatically.

'You never know.' Sam grinned. 'I haven't heard of any tales. I suppose Jack Price might know but I don't want to go asking him in case he wants to know what my interest is.'

Juno nodded. 'See what you mean. What happens now, you open the gate and we go into that space?'

'That's all there is to it.' Sam smiled. 'Come on, then, and keep close behind me.'

As they emerged out of the dunes, Juno dropped the deckchair she had been carrying and stared ahead.

'Christ alive. Will you look at that. My eyes tell me one thing, but I can't believe this is true. This is what I saw last night?' Juno said breathlessly.

'Yes, just look at that sea and sky. Have you ever seen anything like it? It seems vast.' Sam laughed.

Juno sniffed the air.

'Smells like seaside. Must be real, or this is the best illusion I have ever been in.'

Sam smiled as he spread a rug out on the sand. 'Just how many illusions have you been in, then?'

'Ha Ha, comedian,' Juno retorted. 'I suppose you're used to this if you've been lots of times before?'

'Not lots of times, but yes, it's mostly the same whenever I come. Might be a cloud or two, but no rain or cold, so far.'

Juno took off her hat and sunglasses and let the warm breeze bathe her face and ruffle her hair.

'This really is incredible. Have you ever been out swimming here?' Juno nodded towards the waves lapping the beach.

'No, too cautious so far. I don't know whether there are any currents, or surprises. I did poke the water with a stick when I first came, just to see if it might have been acid, or something else.'

Juno laughed.

'Well, you never know,' said Sam, as he sat down on the rug.

'You're not just going to sit there, are you?' Juno smiled. 'We could go for a paddle if nothing else.' She pulled off her trainers and stuffed her white socks in them. 'Come on.' She moved towards the water and held out a hand towards Sam.

'Oh, alright, then.' Sam stood up and slipped off his boots and turned up the legs of his jeans. Juno was standing just at the water's edge.

'Go on. You first,' she urged.

'Guest's privilege, to try the facilities out first.' Sam laughed.

'Coward.' Juno grinned. She put a foot into the water and doubled up with a scream.

Sam raced to her side as she stood up and roared with laughter. 'You should see your face. You've gone as white s a sheet.'

'You utter git,' said Sam with a laugh, picking Juno bodily up and dropping her down as she wriggled and screamed. 'You nearly gave me a heart attack.'

Sam bent down and cupped his hands in the water and threw some at Juno, who yelled out and scampered off back to the rug and threw herself down. Sam followed and looked at the splash marks on Juno's shirt. 'Well, it doesn't look like acid after all. Though it might take time to act.' He knelt beside Juno. 'You know you said I didn't look like a murderer. How do you know what one looks like?'

Juno stared at Sam for a split second and then smiled. 'I think you're okay.' She sat up and wrapped her arms around her knees. 'What did you bring in the flask?'

'Just elderflower again. I must get something else in.'

'No, you're alright. I like it.'

'I have brought some chocolate biscuits. We'd better have them before the sun melts the chocolate.' Sam opened the pack and offered one to Juno.

They sat, side by side, munching biscuits and looking out over the flat sea.

'I can't see any monsters out there,' said Juno brushing crumbs from her mouth. 'I feel a walk in the water, if nothing else, to prove that it's not acid. Coming?'

'Why not,' said Sam. They got to their feet and walked slowly into the water.

'This is lovely,' said Juno. 'The water's quite warm. I haven't had a paddle in the sea since I was a little girl.'

'Long time ago, then.' Sam smiled, as Juno pushed against him.

'So quiet too,' said Juno. 'Not even any birds flying about. Just … nothing. Have you had much of a look round?'

'No, I've kept to this immediate area since I had no idea what to expect and didn't want to get into any problems.'

'Why don't we walk down that way for a bit?' Juno waved her arm towards the right. 'See what we can see.'

Sam looked about.

'What?' Juno asked.

'Trying to fix the position, in case we get lost.'

Juno grinned. 'You're very sensible I suppose. I feel that I could walk for ages. What we could do is walk in the damp sand and then follow our footsteps back.'

'Okay, fair enough. If we see any more than ours then we're in trouble.'

'Could be man Friday.' Juno laughed. 'We could be trespassing on his island.'

'If it is an island,' said Sam. 'I hadn't thought of that. Wonder if there's any buried treasure here?'

'Does this place have a name?'

Sam shook his head. 'No idea. Alec didn't leave any notes.'

'Crusoe Land?' Juno suggested. 'That's what we'll call it. Our own private sanctuary.'

'Hopefully without shipwrecks or pirates.' Sam laughed.

Juno stood and looked up and down the beach. 'Race you, then,' and suddenly she took off, with Sam running after. After a hectic pace they stopped and looked back at their tracks.

'Phew, this beach seems to go on forever,' said Juno, gasping. 'I'm out of condition.'

'Me too,' said Sam, breathing heavily. 'We'd better go back and try and see what's inland.'

Juno nodded and they walked back the way they had come.

The sun was dipping towards the horizon as Juno threw herself down on the rug and searched round for the flask. 'Want some?' She held up a beaker as Sam nodded. Juno drained her cup and then spread herself out on the rug and stared up at the blue sky. Sam settled down beside her.

After a while Juno propped herself up on an elbow, head resting on a hand.

'You were grinning. What's amusing you?'

Sam opened his eyes and looked at Juno.

'You won't believe it, but something came into my head for no reason whatsoever.'

'Come on.' Juno smiled. 'What is it?'

'I suddenly remembered, being a child and sat in Harry Bishop's barber shop over the road from home. Little old Harry, slightly bent, remains of grey hair, never said much and always did the same short back and sides for everyone that I could see. It was a tiny shop, with three metal customer seats, well-worn red plastic seat covers, the stuffing of which had flattened out over time and one barber's chair. Blokes that came in would read the papers in silence, while Harry snipped away. I remember the shelves in the wall in front of the chair. What stood out for me was a bottle with a picture on it. I can't think what the picture was, but I always remember the words over it. Bay Rum. I couldn't understand why Harry had a bottle of rum in his shop and thought that he must take a swig every so often. Not that I really knew what rum was then.'

'Is it a drink, then?'

'No, splash it all over job, sort of after shave. Now why did I think of that, here and now?'

'No idea,' said Juno as she stretched her long legs out and yawned.

'What can you recall of childhood?' Sam asked.

Juno thought for a moment. 'Granny Alice in the back garden of her house. Granny had an old wooden clothes horse that she would put on its side and cover with an old brown blanket. One hot day I was lying in there pretending that it was a tent. I was reading a book. *Exmoor Lass* it was called. A hardback book, with a white horse on the front cover. It might have been my mother's when she was a child. Lovely woman Granny Alice. So kind and interesting.'

'Curious what we can remember,' said Sam. 'I think I read that memories when recalled aren't the re-run of an old tape, but that for a moment, you are actually re-living the event. Don't know if that's true though.'

'We can ask for that past moment,' said Juno wistfully. 'But we can never go back. It's such a shame. Anyway, this is all I need at this time, a place where I can switch off and not think about anything.'

'Nathan you mean?'

Juno groaned. 'Don't spoil it by mentioning him. I know something's got to be done. I can't go on living with him. He scares me.'

'Then it's time you left him.'

'Question is, where do I go? I've lost contact with the friends I once had. No particular skills, except cooking and the odd flower arranging. No family to support me.'

'You have me,' said Sam softly. 'I'll help you all I can.'

'You're very kind, Sam.' Juno reached out and held one of his hands. 'I wouldn't want to cause any trouble for you. I know what Nathan's like.'

'I think I can take care of Nathan in a strop.' Sam smiled. 'He doesn't frighten me.'

'Then I think you should fear him,' said Juno sadly. 'He wouldn't do the dirty work himself, but he has many powerful friends who, no doubt, know somebody who could do whatever was necessary.'

'Really?' Sam questioned.

'Don't underestimate him, Sam, and besides ...' Juno fell silent.

'Besides what?'

'Why would you want to help me? We hardly know each other. I'm not blind, Sam. I've seen those tender looks you give me when you think I don't notice. I don't want you to fall for me any more than I want to fall for you. Not with all this background crap going on. I think I'm damaged goods and you don't deserve that.'

'I don't see you like that at all. I do think you look gorgeous; I can't help feeling that, but I also want to know you better. I think you haven't been loved for a long time and that you could do with some protection and tenderness.'

'What about you, Sam? Your girlfriend, Ellie wasn't it? She dumped you, are you over her?'

Sam reached for Juno's hand. 'Scout's honour. I'm over her. I surprised myself how quickly I did get over her. I thought I was happy enough, but maybe I wasn't, just rubbing along in neutral.'

'I don't see you as a scout somehow.' Juno laughed as she wiped away a tear that had fallen down her cheek.

'Well, I wasn't actually, but I might have been a contender! I do know a couple of knots.' Sam grinned and then said seriously, 'I don't see myself as a rescuer of a glamorous vision, Juno. It's your personality I want, even when you're like a million dollars. All green and wrinkled.'

'Looks are superficial,' said Juno with a smile. 'I just inherited good bone structure, simple really.'

Sam straightened up and looked out over the sea. 'I think, Juno, we should be going home now. I don't want you under any more pressure than you are already.'

Juno smiled and said nothing. She shook out and folded the rug and then looked up at the sky. 'Do you think it's the same sun as we have?'

'Could be. I don't know.' Sam glanced up and down the beach as he collapsed the deckchair. 'Let's go.'

Later that evening, Sam sat in the dark living room at Glebe

Cottage and reflected upon the events of the day. He remembered over and again how he'd assured Juno of his friendship and help and that she had held his hand and briefly kissed him on the cheek. 'Thank you for today,' she'd said simply and then had gone back to the house she shared with an abusive man. Sam thought long and hard until he fell asleep in the chair.

10

The next two days dragged heavily for Sam. He paced round the cottage, trying to find things to do and had fiddled aimlessly in the garden. Once he saw the red sports car come down the road and knew that Nathan was back at the house. No word from Juno and he didn't like to text or email in case Nathan was reading her messages. His head felt like it was going round and round thinking about her, until it made him feel worn out. He knew that he had strong feelings for her but didn't want to be too expressive in case it frightened her away. The very last thing Juno needed was Sam getting all serious with Nathan on the scene.

The sun was dipping down over Anwin Hill as Sam sat in a deckchair in the rear garden, holding a cool can of beer. He marvelled at the view above, golden rays seemed to emanate from the sun and spread across the sky in a manner just like he had once seen on the front cover of some very old magazines from the 1930s that Alec had shown him, many years ago. The sound of running feet crunching on gravel shook Sam out of his reverie and made him sit up. Juno came flying round the corner of the cottage. He shot up out of the chair.

'Juno, what on earth …?' He took in Juno's strange appearance. A long plain navy blue silk evening dress, with a long ragged tear on one side, under an old green fleece and on her feet what looked like battered leather gardening shoes, with laces loosely tied. Juno's hair had been piled up but was coming adrift and wisps of blonde hair fell over her face.

'Run,' Juno yelled, fear in her voice as she bent over, breathing heavily.

'Run, from what?'

'It's Nathan and he's brought someone, Malik … Quickly, they'll find out that I've got out. We must get away.' Juno stood up and grasped both of Sam's arms. 'Sam, come on, we have to move now!'

'I'll ring the police,' said Sam, as he fumbled for his mobile in his jeans pocket. 'What's been going on?'

'No time,' Juno pleaded. 'It'll take far too long for anyone to get here, even if they believe me, which I doubt.'

Sam moved towards the cottage. 'We'll get the car out and drive somewhere where Nathan can't find you.'

Juno nodded and then froze at the sound of a powerful car engine in the road. The noise cut out as the car screeched to a halt outside Glebe Cottage.

'Jesus Christ,' Juno moaned. 'They're here already. Run, we have to run.' She turned and ran up the garden, with Sam following. 'Juno, hold up … where are you going?'

'Where they can't find us,' Juno shouted over her shoulder as she pelted out of the garden and into the field beyond. Sam heard a shout behind and glanced back as he followed her. It was Nathan Randall and with him was a small, slim man, with cropped dark hair and sunglasses. His casual black jeans and cream jacket looked very expensive. Another taller, heavily built man appeared from behind and pulled something from the inside of his jacket pocket. The slim man cautioned him with a swift hand movement and whatever it was went back into the pocket.

Sam caught up with Juno at the dolmen. They stood, breathing heavily. 'Who the fuck are they?' Sam gasped.

'The small guy is a friend of Nathan's, he's called Malik. The other is just security.'

'Security?' Sam's eyebrows shot up. 'This Malik has security?'

'He's something very big in Qatar, where Nathan does a lot of his business now.'

They stood in silence next to the dolmen, under the cover of the trees as they watched the three men emerge from the cottage garden.

They stood still for a moment and then one of them pointed across the field towards the trees that sheltered Sam and Juno.

'They're coming,' Juno cried out.

'We could get round the back of the dolmen and follow the ridge up to Anwin Hill,' suggested Sam. 'It'll take them a while to work it out. We know the land and they don't.'

Juno shook her head. 'The security guy is ex-military and according to Nathan is very good at his job. They'd soon catch us.'

'Look Juno, why don't you just run off and I'll try to hold them up,' said Sam.

Juno gave a thin smile. 'Don't imagine that they'd have a pleasant chat with you about where I'd gone. They've seen me and wouldn't have any scruples about getting you to tell them whatever they want to know.'

They watched as the men spread out slightly and began walking forward across the field.

'Only thing for it, then,' said Sam as he yanked open the iron gate. 'Come on.' He grabbed Juno's hand and pulled her through before slamming the gate shut.

It was dark and windy amongst the dunes. Clouds scudded across the face of the moon, but there was sufficient light to just about see where they were going. Juno headed for the beach when Sam caught hold of her arm. 'Hang on, Juno. If they follow us through, they'll see us easily enough on the beach. There's no cover. Our best bet is to strike inland and try to find cover until dawn. Then we can see better where we are and think of a course of action.'

They threaded their way through the seemingly endless dunes, with grass appearing to become thicker as they went on. As they reached the top of a high dune, Juno peered ahead.

'Look, a light.'

Sam followed where she was pointing and saw two yellow lights, not far ahead. 'Might be a place we can hide in,' said Sam.

It took them longer to reach than they'd thought as they weaved through the steep dunes but, at last, they reached a strange, square looking building. There was a large bronze coloured metal door in the face of what seemed to be a dark green painted concrete wall. The wall looked to be higher than they had first thought and they stood in front of the otherwise featureless wall and wondered what to do next.

'Looks like a fort, or something,' suggested Sam. 'No windows, looks more like a defensive structure.'

'We can't stay here, I'm chilling off,' said Juno as she walked up to the door and hammered on it with her fist. Nothing happened, so Juno and Sam banged again. This time, after a while, the door opened slightly and a small, pale face with receding grey hair peeped round with eyes wide open, staring at them in surprise.

'Who are you and how did you come to be here?' The face spoke with a low voice. 'The ships have gone, none are left.'

'We came through … well … from somewhere else,' said Sam. 'We don't know how we came to be here but there are some people after us and they may follow us here. We need help, somewhere to hide from them,' said Sam as he looked at Juno.

The door opened a little more and a light came on inside to reveal a large hallway. They could see more clearly that the person before them was a little thin man, dressed in a long black tunic over black trousers with what looked like red slippers on his feet. The smooth skinned face was edged with a neatly trimmed grey beard and Sam was relieved to see that the man's brown eyes while appearing wary were also friendly enough.

'I do not know about anything you speak of,' said the man. 'You had better come in and Lady Maeven will decide what is best to be done.' The man stood aside to admit Sam and Juno into the building and then closed the door behind them.

'Please wait here,' said the man, who then ascended, without haste, a long flight of wooden stairs running up one side of the wall. Sam and Juno looked about what they assumed was a large entrance hall, painted in a pale yellow, with a great glass chandelier suspended centrally from the white plaster ceiling. Sam tapped the old wooden planks of the floor with his shoe.

'Interesting, looks like old ships timbers.' Sam then went over to a large chest placed against one of the walls. It looked to be very old, made of a dark wood and carved in minute detail, showing some fantastic scene that depicted a winged dragon fighting a sea serpent. On another wall hung an enormous colourful tapestry of great age that showed a city of white buildings near a coastline. Sam indicated two high back wooden chairs that flanked the wall furthest from them that contained closed double doors of lightly tanned wood. 'Might as well sit down. We don't know how long he's going to be.'

'I do hope he's locked the door,' said Juno. 'What happens if Nathan and his mates turn up?'

'We don't know for sure that they've seen us go through the gate,' said Sam. 'I'm hoping they might take a look and bugger off, searching for us in the wrong place and that we can sneak back home after a while. Lord knows what this place is and who's here. I think I'd feel happier if we got going as soon as it appears safe.'

Juno looked doubtful.

'Anyway,' said Sam with a half-smile, 'what's with the fashion statement?' He inclined his head towards Juno's dress, with the long tear. Juno looked down.

'Damn it. I think I must have caught it on the window catch when I climbed out.'

'Climbed out? What happened?' Sam smiled.

'It's not funny, Sam,' Juno scolded. 'I was terrified. I had to do something. I said I was feeling ill and needed to dash to the loo. I suppose they thought I couldn't go anywhere and just laughed and then agreed. Once in there I quickly climbed out of the window, lucky for me it's on the ground floor. Got out and ran past the back garage, which has a gardening store at the end. I ran in, grabbed the fleece and my old gardening shoes. I knew I couldn't run in the heels I had on and then ran across the lawn and squeezed through the hedge before coming to you.'

'Bloody hell, Juno,' said Sam. 'You've had a helluva time.' He peered closely at Juno's face and gently pushed aside a lock of her hair to expose a red blotch on the side of her cheek. 'Nathan I assume?' Sam said angrily.

'Yes, it was awful. I've never been so afraid. Luckily, I managed to keep it together and get away. Otherwise, God knows what would have happened.' Juno wrapped her arms around her body and looked as if she would burst into tears. Just then, the sound of footsteps and the small man descended the stairs. 'Lady Maeven will see you. Please follow me.'

11

Sam and Juno entered a large, square room of a pale burnt orange colour, with a white ceiling and a similar chandelier to the one in the hall. One face of the room was taken up by what looked like a great glass sliding door that appeared to give onto an open outside space. A huge, pale wooden bookcase stood against another wall, filled with books of all sizes and in what seemed a haphazard manner. Four large white porcelain-looking vases, decorated with colourful images of mystical creatures from some unrecognisable mythology stood at each corner of the room. A long wooden table stood in the centre of the room, set about with delicately carved wooden chairs. At the furthest end of the room stood a very tall lady of slender build, with a lightly tanned face and long grey braided hair swept back from her face and falling down her back. She wore a long, off white linen dress and several fine gold chains round her neck and finely wrought golden bracelets on her wrists. Any apprehension that Sam and Juno felt was dissolved by the friendly smile and the gentle blue eyes that gazed upon them for a moment. The woman gave a few touches to the arrangement of blue and yellow flowers that stood in a tall bronze vase in front of her.

'I am Maeven. Who are you and where can you have possibly come from? You don't look like City dwellers.'

'I'm Sam and this is Juno.' Sam smiled back. 'We're not certain exactly how we came to be here but our home village is Sheriford, which is not far from Salisbury and then by going through a gate in a dolmen in Uncle Alec's field we found that we ... simply arrived here.'

To Sam's relief Maeven did not react as if she were listening to the babble of a dangerous lunatic but gave a light laugh and held up a hand.

'What a strange tale. I have heard that such travellings were possible, but to have arrived here at … such an unfortunate time for us. Still, you look as if your journey has been an arduous one.' Maeven smiled at Juno, who looked down at her torn and somewhat grubby dress and scruffy shoes. Maeven then turned towards the small man, who had remained quietly by the entrance door.

'Jon, would you please show our guests to one of the living rooms and let them select some garments if they wish and then we'll have dinner out on the terrace. Go with Jon, he will help you.'

'Just one thing,' said Juno as she turned to go. 'We came here to escape three men who wish to harm us. I wouldn't want to bring any trouble to you but it may be that they've followed us here. We'll leave if you wish but would be grateful if you could show us a safe way from here.'

'Indeed?' Maeven raised an eyebrow. 'Have you come from the City?'

'No, we came from some place out along the beach, amongst all the dunes. I'm not too sure that we could find out way back, at least in the dark.'

'Ah, yes. It is easy to get lost there,' said Maeven. 'The dunes are extensive. If these people followed you they may find it not at all easy to discover you. Jon, would you please take such measures as you think fit? Thank you.'

'I will ensure that all doors are secured now my Lady,' said Jon. He turned towards Sam and Juno. 'If you would follow me, I will show you to a living room.'

They walked along a wide corridor with plain pink walls and a light coloured parquet wood floor and stopped before the first of a line of closed wooden doors.

'These are the rooms once occupied by Lady Maeven's family,' said Jon as he pushed open the door to reveal a large square room, this time of pale green walls. There were tall windows on one face, partially draped by brightly pattered curtains. A long wooden cabinet, richly carved, stood along one wall and in the centre of the room worn brown leather easy chairs were placed around a low wooden table with a pale marble top.

'Through here,' said Jon moving across to another door in one of the walls, 'are the bedrooms and clothing cupboards.' He stood at the door and opened it. 'Inside and to the right is a room where you can bathe if you wish. I will leave you now and will return when dinner is ready.'

Sam and Juno walked into a large bedroom; pale red curtains drawn across a window. A wide bed stood against one wall with pastel coloured sheets, blankets and pillows all neatly in place. A large carpet configured with bright abstract patterns covered much of the wooden floor. Juno crossed over to a long, low wall shelf, with a mirror attached and peered at the glass.

'Ugh, just as well you didn't tell me what I looked like.' She grinned.

A small padded wooden seat had been placed under the shelf and in front of the mirror.

'I suppose this is a lady's dressing table,' mused Juno as she opened a couple of small drawers that hung under the shelf. She picked out a dark green glass bottle, cautiously unscrewed the silver top and sniffed. 'Wow, what a lovely scent. This can here looks like it might be talc.'

'Let's check the clothing cupboards,' suggested Sam.

After a rummage amongst the clothes hanging in the cupboards, Juno held up a beautiful knee length dress made from a silky material. 'This feels gorgeous. Look at the decorations, all those small embroidered stars and flowers. It must have taken ages to make. What do you think?' She looked enquiringly. 'Looks like it might fit.'

'I've found some chino type trousers and a baggy black shirt that looks mediaeval,' called Sam as he rustled through the clothes. 'Even a couple of pairs of socks.'

'No bras, but looks like I'm in luck for new knickers.' Juno smiled as she held up a pair of black lacy boy shorts.

'Do you want a shower first?' Sam called out. He stood in the doorway of a large, tiled room. 'There's a loo, massive basin, shower, everything, even shower gel. Can't believe it, it's like being in a posh hotel.'

'Yes, I'll go first if that's okay,' said Juno as she laid her haul of clothes on the bed. 'I feel sweaty and dirty, a clean-up and a hair wash will be great.'

Juno experimented with the shower controls and found an extractor fan switch while Sam located interior lights on an outside wall switch.

After a lot of splashing, Juno emerged, clad in a large soft yellow bath towel, rubbing her wet hair with a smaller towel.

'Your go, Sam. Wonder if there's a hairdryer in here?' Juno looked in the shelf drawers.

'No, too much to hope for I suppose. Odd thing is, Sam, for a moment in the shower I forgot why and how we came here.' Juno frowned as she towelled her hair. 'I wonder whether they followed us, it's all so unreal.'

Sam smiled as he headed for the shower. 'I know what you mean. All of this puts you off your guard. Maeven seems okay, but this place is, well, I don't know. It feels as if something's not right.'

Washed and refreshed and clad in new clean clothes Sam and Juno pulled back the curtains and stood at the window, looking out across the dark sea, when Jon tapped discreetly on the door and announced that dinner was served on the terrace.

Jon led the way back to the room where they had first met Maeven and indicated that they should pass through the open sliding doors. Sam and Juno found themselves out on a big square paved area, edged with a low wall of honey coloured stone. A long wooden table stood in the centre of the space and three chairs, each facing each other had been placed at one end of the table. Cutlery and fine white china plates had been set for three persons. In the centre of the table stood two large silver candelabra, the candles gave off a soft flickering yellow light. A warm breeze came in from the sea. Maeven stood at the end of the table and indicated that Sam and Juno should be seated. Jon then appeared pushing a trolley laden with covered silver dishes, which he placed upon the table before withdrawing.

'It's ridiculous,' said Maeven, smiling. 'The number of times I've invited him to dine with me, but he can never bring himself to do it. Don't know why, but he seems to want to preserve the status quo, which is silly, especially now. Anyway, come and help yourselves. There are hot, boiled potatoes, vegetables, fresh bread and our special cheese, oh and some boiled eggs. It's a bit of a mixture, but it's been a long time since we have had anyone to dine here and supplies are a bit low. Now, you must try the wine.' Maeven picked up a black bottle from the table and poured a pale liquid into three cut glass goblets and passed them round. 'It's rather fine and not much of it left. Used to be produced up in the hills where the soil is particularly good for this grape variety. Your health,' said Maeven as she took a drink. 'Now do help yourselves and don't look so apprehensive.' Maeven laughed. 'At least you've found some clean clothes. That dress looks lovely on you, Juno.'

'Thank you, it fits really well and I was also lucky to find some suede ankle boots that fit. So much better than the gardening shoes I arrived in.'

'Gardening shoes?' Maeven smiled.

'Yes, I had to come away in great haste and they were all that was to hand,' said Juno as she helped herself to potatoes and vegetables.

Maeven sat back in her chair and drank from her goblet. 'I don't wish to pry, but you can appreciate that I'm curious as to how and why you have arrived at my home in some state and talking of pursuit by three men, I think you said.'

Juno nodded. 'It's me they're after, not Sam, he's been trying to help me.' She paused and smiled at Sam. 'Thank goodness he has otherwise I hate to think what might have happened to me.'

'Yes,' said Sam. 'What did provoke you into running to my place?'

'Nathan came back and said he wanted dinner prepared because Malik was coming later. He seemed very on edge and I asked him what was wrong. You have no idea, he told me and then lost it completely. I couldn't believe what I was hearing. Nathan was always so in control, but not now. He was in a panic and went on about how he was deeply in with Malik over some devious arms deal in the Middle East. Apparently, it had gone badly wrong and they had lost a huge amount of money due to one of Nathan's friends, who'd been involved, pulling out at the last minute. Malik had been very angry and said that Nathan had cost him a lot of money.'

'What sort of sum?' Sam asked as he finished his wine.

'Millions. He couldn't make good the loss and Malik was not the sort of man to tolerate any failure that affected him. Nathan said that he had previously transferred a large sum into my name, to hide it from the Inland Revenue and now needed it transferred back to help him pay off Malik. He said that I had to sign some legal form of transfer. Then he said I'd better get dressed as Malik would be arriving soon. So, you can imagine as I was getting ready my head was in a turmoil. Then, just as I came downstairs, Malik arrived with one of his security guards and looked me over. Made my flesh crawl. He said to Nathan, "have you told her?" "No," said Nathan, "I haven't had the time." Malik gave some sort of contemptuous look at Nathan and said to me. "Your husband doesn't value you at all. Do you know what he has done?"

'No, I said, but he was telling me about some deal with you that has gone wrong and cost you a lot of money.'

Malik had nodded and said that it was so, but by way of some redress, Nathan had agreed that in future I would belong to Malik.

That Malik and I would fly that night to Qatar where I would …
God knows what. I appealed to Nathan, unable to comprehend what
was happening. He just stood there and said nothing, looking both
desperate and relieved at the same time. Malik obviously had no time
for Nathan and he said that Nathan was no man just to give his wife
away to another. Malik said that, in essence, he had long fancied
me and that Nathan's financial problems gave Malik the leverage he
needed to get me.'

'Jesus,' Sam breathed. 'I had no idea it could be so bad.'

'Luckily for me I kept my head, despite what I'd heard and like I
told you, Sam, I asked to go to the loo as I was feeling sick. That smug
bastard Malik said that while the news must be a surprise, I would
soon recover and recognise that he could offer me a much better
situation with him than Nathan. I played it a bit cool and headed
off and as soon as I was in there climbed straight out of the window
and then came to you.' Juno smiled at Sam. 'That's the whole story.'

'What a terrible story,' said Maeven, looking shocked. 'I'd like to
be able to offer you sanctuary for as long as you need it. However,
circumstances do not permit. I think that it would be best if you
returned to your own world in the morning.'

Juno looked anxious. 'I don't think Nathan, at least, would give
up until he has the transfer signed and I don't know about Malik.'

'Is there anywhere else here we could go?' Sam asked. 'At least for
a few days.'

Maeven looked thoughtful and then stood up. 'I would love to be
able to help you, if I could. Look, come over here, I have something
to show you.'

Maeven crossed to one of the corners of the stone wall and pointed
into the distance.

'Look over there.'

Sam and Juno stood next to Maeven and followed the line of
her outstretched finger. A large city stood illuminated by a myriad

of lights. They could see tall buildings and what looked like rows of houses. Cranes stood next to a large port area of docks and warehouses and further to the left a large tube-like structure stood in an open space.

'It's simply called the City,' said Maeven sadly. 'It's been here for well over a thousand years. Originally a trading port, but latterly as well for cargo ships that fly the line between Cynus and Etheron.'

'Are those other cities?' Sam asked. 'Perhaps we could go there?'

Maeven smiled. 'No, they are galaxies.'

Sam whistled and looked incredulous. 'We have nothing like this at home.'

Maeven bent down and picked up a brown canvas bag that lay at her feet and pulled out what looked like a laptop and tapped the screen. 'The City is fully automated. From this device I can activate the power station and turn on all the lights in the public areas. I like to light it up at night. It gives the impression that the place is still being lived in. All that life that has existed for so long.' Maeven sighed.

'What's wrong?' Sam asked, uneasily.

'In a short while, it will all be destroyed.' Maeven looked gaunt and turned away from the view of the glittering city.

12

Sam and Juno stood in shocked silence, unable to think of anything meaningful to say. Sam had a sinking feeling that things might not be going to work out well for Juno and himself. Maeven leaned against a wall, as she stared at the City again.

'You know, my late husband Valeran and I were Grand Councillors of the place. For over sixty years we were elected to the positions. Not a huge amount to do as the place virtually ran itself. But the titles carried a certain cachet, shall we say. Trade came in and went out. Everyone seemed prosperous and content, no social troubles. Then, some time ago we had news of the Nivar. A ruthless band of destroyers from beyond the Twelve Stars. I think the tyrant in charge calls himself the High Lord. He basically operates as the chief of a band of quasi-religious lunatics, who view it as their ordained task to take over as much of the universe as they can. Obviously for their own benefit. They are well equipped and powerful, though why they should want to come and destroy a quiet backwater like the City I can't understand. Probably just because it exists.'

'So, the Nivar are on their way here now?' Sam asked slowly.

'Yes.'

'When?'

'Soon,' said Maeven. 'That's why I didn't want you to stay. You have to go back to where you came from, before the Nivar arrive.'

'What about the people in the City?' Juno asked. 'What will happen to them?'

Maeven gave a thin smile. 'Fortunately, we received early warning of the Nivar advance and were able to put arrangements in place. They had stopped off to destroy a planet in the Serras Quadrant and apparently it took them a lot longer than they had thought it would and cost them a great number of casualties. But you see the City is really only a trading port, although the largest and wealthiest. We are on one of the four great islands on a planet covered with water. The people of the City were evacuated on a fleet of transports and cruisers two weeks ago. They are heading for the Denamar galaxy, where there is a federation of authorities who, hopefully, might be able to put enough force together to provide a defence. The other islands here don't have sufficient wealth to make them worthy of attack by the Nivar, well, that is what I hope.'

'But you and Jon are still here,' said Sam. 'Why didn't you leave with the rest of the people?'

Maeven looked past Sam, out towards the dark sky and the clouds floating past the brilliant silver moon. 'Valeran died three years ago. My children are all grown and have their own children and responsibilities to them. They have no need of me, despite what they said. That's one of the great sadnesses of growing old. No one has need of you anymore, you slip quietly into becoming an object, to be picked up and put down and considered as an afterthought. Of course, my children made a great fuss about me staying here, but I knew that I wasn't needed and parted with them, but with a heavy heart that I kept to myself. My biggest regret is that Jon wouldn't go. He insisted on staying with me. He's been with me since he was a child and says that he has no family who care for him and nowhere to go and if the journey is to end, he would like to remain with me. Astonishing, isn't it? Makes me feel quite humble.' Maeven drew herself up to her full height.

'Besides,' she said with a grim smile, 'Jon and I have work yet to do. There was a concern that the Nivar could track the course of the evacuation to Denamar and pursue them. In the City are a number of defensive rocket batteries, installed years ago, when times were less settled. When news of the Nivar broke, much work was undertaken to ensure that the batteries would still function. The Nivar might find something of a surprise when they arrive. Jon and I might even end up as heroes, although probably dead ones. Just so long as there is no pursuit.'

'Why not just leave with us and come back into our world?' Juno suggested. 'Why does it have to end here for you?'

'Because it does,' said Maeven wearily. 'I hate to think what Valeran would make of it all. In an awful sense, I am glad that he is not alive to see what's coming. I have always lived here, what would I do for a few more years in your world? However, I thank you for your consideration.' They stood together, looking out at the City, unable to say anything more.

'You must be very tired,' said Maeven. 'Why not go and get some rest. I can see that Juno has been yawning.'

'It's been an incredible day and that's an understatement,' said Juno, as she yawned again. 'I hate it when that happens. Once I start yawning, I find it hard to stop.'

As they left the room, Sam and Juno looked back at Maeven, standing still and looking at the City.

'God, this is terrible, Sam. I hate to think what will happen to her and Jon.'

'Yes, but we must think about what we should do next, since hiding out here isn't an option.'

Sam was wondering how to deal with the bed situation as he washed his face. When he came out of the shower room, the ceiling lights were dim and he could see Juno lying on the bed, fully dressed. He crept closer and saw her eyes closed and breathing evenly and smiled. Sam gently draped a large blanket over Juno's curled body and retired to one of the easy chairs. With the information he had just absorbed, he didn't see himself being able to sleep easily as his head ran over possible scenarios of what to do next.

Sam registered a touch on his hand and panicked as he woke. He jerked up, wincing at the stiffness in his neck. He must have been asleep after all. The room was mostly in darkness, lit only by moonlight visible through the slightly open curtains.

'What's up?' Sam grunted, as he massaged his neck. He was suddenly aware of Juno standing over him, naked, save for her boy shorts. 'I woke up and you looked so uncomfortable there. Come to bed. It's big enough.' Juno gently took hold of Sam's hand and helped him upright. He quickly threw off his clothes and sank gratefully under the sheets and blankets. They clasped hands briefly and then sank into a deep sleep.

13

The bedclothes seemed to have, somehow, wrapped themselves round him during the night. Sam could see sunlight streaming in between the curtains and then glanced at the lump of blankets and sheets that mostly covered Juno. Her breathing was deep and regular and Sam thought she must still be asleep. He felt a warm glow inside at the realisation that he had woken up in the same bed as Juno, despite the peculiar circumstances of their situation. He found it a moment to be savoured. One of Juno's bare shoulders peeped out from the covering of sheets and Sam resisted an urge to gently caress her skin. After a while, he forced himself out from the web of bedclothes and picked up his clothes that he had tossed on the floor the night before. He moved towards the shower when he heard Juno give a sigh and struggle against the sheets that covered her. She raised herself up on one elbow, peering through a mess of hair.

'What time is it?'

Sam smiled. 'No idea, I'm afraid. Needless to say my phone is useless but from the sunlight coming in, I would say that it was late morning.'

'Wonderful.' Juno grunted and sank back down. 'What are you up to?'

'Going to have a Welsh vegetable.' Sam laughed.

'A what?'

'A leak.'

'Oh, very amusing and so early too.' Juno frowned with mock irritation.

'I'll get ready and then go and find Maeven,' said Sam. 'I suppose we had better get ready to move out today.'

A while later, Sam found Maeven standing at the table of what he thought of as the 'burnt orange' room.

'Sleep well?' Maeven enquired.

'Very well indeed. Thank you,' Sam replied. 'I hadn't realised how tired I was.'

'Juno well?'

'Yes, I think she's taking a bit longer to surface.' Sam smiled.

'Good. Things to do today, but first I'll ask Jon to get us something to eat.'

Jon had provided a breakfast of warm, crusty rolls, fruit, honey and cheese, together with a flask of what tasted like strong coffee. Juno walked in, with a swish of her black dress, hair combed and looking fresh and well rested. 'Good morning.' She smiled.

'Hmm, this is good,' said Sam, as he drank from his cup.

'It's called Kres,' said Maeven. 'Locally made and certainly does wake you up.'

'Just in time for breakfast.' Sam smiled as Juno sat down at the table.

'Great. I'm famished.'

Appetites satisfied, they sat back in their chairs. Maeven stood up and leaned on the table, as if she had something to say, when Sam noticed a tall, thin white light out on the terrace area where they had dined the night before. 'What on earth is that?' Sam pointed.

Maeven twisted round and gasped in horror.

'Nivar, they are here sooner than I calculated.'

The light moved slowly into the room as Sam and Juno scrambled to their feet and with Maeven shrank towards the door. Then the light seemed to thin and slowly assume a humanoid form, before transforming into a tall, well-built, middle-aged man, with a strong face and trimmed brown hair. He was dressed in what looked like a working overall of khaki colour, with many pockets. His pale blue eyes looked carefully at each of them in turn. They were ready to bolt if he made an aggressive move. Finally, the figure smiled and held his hands open.

'I am Leossamanath. I know it's a bit of a mouthful. Most call me Leo. I'm sorry if I have surprised you.'

Faced with this disarming admission, Maeven took a step forward and drew herself up.

'I am Maeven, and this is Sam and Juno. You don't look like what I assume Nivar to be. Who are you?'

'No, I am not Nivar. We know of them and have been following their movements for some time.'

'Then, who are you? Where do you come from? How did you get here?' Maeven asked briskly. 'All of the others in the City have left.'

'Yes, I am aware of that too. To start with, I should say that I have assumed a humanoid form on the basis that your senses will be able and happy to communicate with me. So much easier if you're not terrified of the sight of what is in front of you.' Leo grinned. 'I am what you could call one of the Ancients. There have been other names in the past. Watchers, Guardians, Keepers and other things, but Ancients is the title that seems to stick.' Leo paused and looked at the remains of the meal on the table. 'I appear to have interrupted your meal.'

'Forgive my manners,' said Maeven. 'Can I offer you something?'

'Oh no, very kind, but we have no need for food or drink to sustain us. It's just that some of it looks and smells delicious. It's almost a shame that we don't need such things. To answer your question, where have I come from? I can say that I have come from here and there and other places, immeasurably far away and near all at once.'

'That sounds hard to comprehend,' said Sam. 'I think I'll need another cup of Kres, or even something stronger to help deal with that notion.'

Leo walked round for a moment, deep in thought. Then he

stopped and faced Sam.

'Basically, I and others like me are just pure thought. We once had a bodily form, similar to yours, but evolved away from the need for such physical covering, with all its distracting faults and defects.'

'Pure thought?' Maeven asked. 'How long did it take to gain that state?'

'Billions of years,' said Leo.

'Even before Big Bang, then?' Sam asked eagerly.

'I don't know what this Big Bang is that you refer to,' said Leo.

'It's a theory that the universe resulted from one massive explosive moment and is still, after billions of years, spreading out.'

Juno tried to look interested but said, 'Look, history apart and I'm sure that it's fascinating, but Maeven has said that a group of thugs, called Nivar are coming here to invade and destroy the place. Sam and I must get back to our world as soon as possible.'

'That,' beamed Leo, 'is in a sense why I am here. It's because of you two. You shouldn't be here.'

'Oh great,' said Sam. 'I should tell you that we didn't exactly come here from our own choice but are trying to escape from some unpleasant people who wish to do us harm.'

'You know, it's very interesting,' mused Leo, 'that you referred to the creation of the universe as you call it. There is, of course, more than one and we Ancients are older than most of them.'

'So, you existed in thought form, at least before the creation of our universe,' said Maeven. 'That's going to take some thinking about, not that we have time for such luxury now.'

'If you're that old,' said Juno, 'presumably you've developed superpowers and could therefore stop this Nivar invasion if you wanted to.'

Maeven shot at glance at Juno and looked hopeful.

Leo breathed in deeply and sighed. 'I'm afraid not. We are under strict laws never to interfere in any of the worlds we visit.'

'So, what's your purpose, then?' Maeven sounded exasperated.

'Well, our purpose if you like is to identify and close any tears, holes or rents, or whatever you want to call it, in the fabric of reality that would enable transfer of bodies between the universal versions.'

'That sounds like a mouthful.' Juno grinned. 'Like something out of Star Wars.'

'How many are there of what you call rents that you have to deal with?' Maeven asked.

'Not too many, fortunately,' Leo replied. 'Take one near here for example.'

'The one down near the beach?' Sam asked. 'That's a rent between universes?'

'Yes.' Leo smiled. 'In essence, it was caused by the collision of two large gas planets, which in turn triggered a catastrophic collision with a very large star, which then, in the resulting chain of explosions, destroyed three galaxies. The resultant, very violent shockwaves have been travelling for billions of years and one last gasp was to cause the rent, or tear if you like, that you've mentioned.'

'So, it hasn't been round forever?'

'No, I suppose some fifty years in your notion of time,' said Leo.

'Hang on,' said Sam. 'You said that you were here to close up tears in whatever this fabric is. Can you hold on until Juno and I get back home?'

'I can allow that easily enough.' Leo smiled. 'Your presence here has not caused any lasting dimensional upset. Besides, I can't close the rent on my own.'

'You need a team of fixers?' Juno laughed. 'Sounds like getting in a firm of plumbers and that's never easy.'

'Only one more,' said Leo. 'I've summoned my partner, Perra, to come here. I'm hoping she will bring a fusion bar with her.'

'What's that for?' Maeven asked.

'It's a specialised instrument that takes our concentrated thought patterns, amplifies them greatly and then seals a rent in the fabric.'

'You need at least two to do this?' Sam asked.

'Yes, Perra is on her way. It can take a very long time for her to get here, depending upon her location.'

'Why?'

'Space is so vast and there are so few of us left to do the work we do. Usually, we are on our own and must summon a meeting to actually effect a seal. We are often spread very far apart.'

'Why is that?' Sam smiled. 'Recruitment problem?'

'Not too far wrong.' Leo shrugged. 'We have existed for so long that some have simply terminated their existence to avoid the endless monotony of time. Others have gone mad and had to be terminated in case they interfered in universal entities. I will tell you that it is refreshing to assume a physical form and to talk to real people, instead of interminable conversations in one's head.'

As Leo finished talking, another white light manifested itself in the room.

'It's Perra. I didn't think she would be here so soon,' Leo called out excitedly. The light was transformed into a well-built, fresh-faced female figure, with long brown hair that flowed around her shoulders. She was clad in a long dress of a shimmering green gold material. The woman gave a brilliant smile as she turned towards Leo. 'Such a long time, Leo. It is good to see you.'

'Perra, most welcome and I am complete now that you are here.' Leo advanced and they embraced. 'I have missed you, Perra,' said Leo. 'Let me introduce you to Maeven, who is an inhabitant of this planet and Sam and Juno who have come through a rent from another dimension. You have brought a fusion bar?' Perra tapped a small black leather bag that hung from a long shoulder strap.

'I have explained that Sam and Juno have to return to their own world before we can close the rent,' said Leo.

Perra frowned. 'I have been made aware of others from the same world who have come here. They must be located and returned as well.'

Sam and Juno exchanged glances. 'Maybe it's Nathan and his mates,' suggested Sam. 'We did tell Leo that we didn't come here exactly from choice. We had to escape harm from what are probably the ones you have mentioned.'

'Not only that,' Maeven interrupted, 'we are expecting an imminent attack from a Nivar war fleet. Thankfully the inhabitants of the City have been evacuated. However, I want to make sure that the Nivar don't attempt a pursuit.'

'A difficult situation, then,' said Perra. 'I had detected a large Nivar vessel approaching. We still have time to close the rent. We cannot afford the Nivar breaking through into another world. The balance would be irrevocably upset.'

At that moment Jon walked through the door and stood stock still, eyes wide open.

'All is well, Jon,' Maeven hastened to reassure him. 'There is no need to be afraid. This is Leo and Perra, who have come to close the dimensional rent.'

'I understand you, my Lady. In all my years I have seen strange sights, but these days …'

'Strange times indeed, Jon,' Maeven said. 'Becoming stranger still. Perra has informed us that there are others from another world here. They must be found and returned, hopefully before the Nivar arrive. Have you seen anyone?'

'No, my Lady, but I must advise you that two of the missile launch keys have shown on my instrument panel as having gone offline. It may be that the keys need replacing. I will return to the City as soon as possible with new ones.'

'Go down to the arsenal and draw out two new keys. There should be some there. But Jon, be especially alert for any Nivar arriving early.'

Jon nodded and with a curious glance at Leo and Perra left the room.

14

They were all standing outside Maeven's house. In the daylight the grassy dunes, stretching away to the right and to the left did not look to Sam to be so forbidding. He glanced up at the smooth windowless walls. 'It looked like a fortress when we first saw your house. Somewhat grim.'

Maeven smiled. 'Well, you're right. It was a fort. A command post in fact. That was many years ago. It was derelict when Valeran purchased it and converted it into our home. We installed all the windows to look out onto the sea. The views, particularly at sunset, are wonderful. I suppose that's why it looks so unwelcoming from the landward side.'

Behind the house, a long gravel track snaked away across rough, flat grassland towards the City, behind which low, dark hills rose in the distance. Maeven kept glancing skywards in anticipation of the Nivar.

Jon had brought round from a small building at the side of the house a sort of electric powered buggy and was loading two pale grey packs into the rear cargo area. Sam and Juno were just standing, looking on, not quite sure what they were supposed to do next. Leo and Perra stood a little way off, talking in low tones. They held one another's hands and were obviously deeply connected with each other.

Everyone froze when Juno screamed. Nathan, Malik and the other man crept round from another side of the house. The security guy holding an automatic pistol.

'There you are at last, you bitch,' Nathan snarled, his clothes stained and dishevelled. 'I don't know what the hell is happening here but at last I've got you and we have unfinished business.'

Sam edged forward to shield Juno from any attack by the clearly angry Nathan.

'Don't think you can beat the hell out of her anymore, you shit,' Sam yelled. 'She's not on her own now.'

'Just who is this?' Maeven asked stonily.

'My husband, Nathan,' said Juno quietly. 'One of the men we're running from.'

Leo and Perra walked closer. 'You are the ones from another world,' said Perra. 'You must all go back now in order that we may seal the rent.' Perra drew a long black tube from her leather bag.

Immediately Malik drew a pistol from an inside pocket of his jacket and pointed it towards Perra.

'No one is going anywhere,' said Malik coldly. 'Not until I know what exactly is going on here. I've managed to convince myself that this is not some kind of peculiar dream.' He nodded towards Juno. 'Certainly, you are part of this, you and your stupid husband.'

Nathan frowned and then stared at Juno. 'I want you to sign this.' He drew a crumpled looking sheet of white paper from his pocket.

'Oh, the famous transfer of funds. At a time like this and in a place like this all you can think of is money.' Juno gave a thin smile. 'It's too ridiculous for words. Do I assume that the rest of the bargain will also fall into place? That I must go with Malik?'

'Well, I don't know what …' Nathan glanced at Malik, who stood looking with contempt.

'You have cost me dearly. Do you think I would be happy to accept your cast off wife? I'm only concerned with getting out of this place.' Moving swiftly, Malik stepped behind Juno and put the muzzle of his pistol against her head.

'I don't think you're taking this seriously. I can see some buildings over there, perhaps a town of sorts. There must be a way by road or rail to where we want to be. I'm not a patient man and I advise you to co-operate, for your own health.'

Malik turned his head in the direction of the security guy.

'Stokes, get her.'

'You're coming with us,' Malik said to Juno. 'A guarantee of our safety.'

'No way,' shouted Sam, as he lunged forward. Stokes easily side stepped an enraged Sam and brought the butt of his pistol down on Sam's head, to send him crashing down to the ground.

'Bastard, you scum,' Juno shrieked and flew at Stokes, who simply punched her in the stomach, leaving Juno doubled up on the ground, gasping for breath.

'Pathetic,' Malik smiled. 'At last we are getting somewhere.' He leaned over Juno. 'You have caused me a great deal of trouble. I should, at this moment, be in Qatar, where I have urgent business. Instead, I have spent time searching the English countryside for you and then went through some form of gate under a group of stones and arrived in a load of sand dunes. I'm not really convinced that any of this is real.' He waved his gun in Juno's face. 'Perhaps I should shoot you, to see what happens.'

'You will not do that,' said Leo sternly.

'I have no idea who, or what you are,' said Malik. 'I advise you to back off. My friends and I are going to that place over there and will take her with us.' He looked at Jon.

'He can drive us in that machine.' Malik acted quickly and bundled Juno into the back of the buggy and told Nathan and Stokes to get in. Malik sat in the front, with his pistol held to Juno's head. 'Now, move this thing.'

Jon looked at Maeven, who gave a brief smile and nodded. Sam was crouched on the ground, cursing. He tried to stand up, holding his head as the buggy sped off in the direction of the City. They stood in shocked silence for a moment, staring after the buggy, then Maeven broke the moment.

'Look,' she said, pointing skywards. A small, dark speck had appeared. 'The Nivar are here,' she said bleakly.

15

S am staggered to his feet and tried to run after the buggy, as it rapidly sped towards the City. He stopped and turned back to Leo.

'Leo, help me,' Sam pleaded. 'I must get to her, or Malik will kill her. I know he will.'

Leo hesitated and looked at Perra

'You know you cannot interfere,' Perra warned.

'Look, you say that you're thought only and have existed for God knows how long. Surely you have some powers that you could use to save a life. I can't see that as interfering.' Sam pointed towards the City. 'When they find that there's no way from there back to our world they'll kill Juno. They'll blame her for it all.'

Leo and Perra stared at each other again, appearing as if they were trying to mentally resolve some great problem.

'For God's sake, do something,' Sam yelled, as he stared at them both. 'Jesus Christ, what is the bloody point of you? Well, fuck you.'

Sam turned and began to run towards the City.

Leo gave a sad smile to Perra. 'I will not cause harm, but I must help Sam release Juno. I can see that in the hearts of those men there is evil and that they will hurt her. I will help Sam and then return. Perra, you go to the rent and await our coming.'

'Very well,' said Perra doubtfully. 'But remember our prime directive to seal the rent and restore balance.'

Leo nodded and in an instant transformed his human aspect into the now familiar white light. It hovered for a moment and flew to catch up with Sam. The light enfolded him and picked him, struggling, off the ground and then vanished towards the City.

'What's that above us?' Nathan asked, as he looked up into the sky. Something dark, too far away to see detail, beyond the fact that it looked like a tube, with ailerons attached, was travelling, high up, towards the City.

Malik glanced up. 'No idea. Let's just concentrate on getting out of here.' He jabbed his pistol into the back of Jon's neck. 'What's up ahead? Looks like some sort of airport.'

'That's the flight deck for the City,' Jon replied. 'The freighters and passenger ships used to arrive and depart from there.'

'Good.' Malik grinned and turned to look at Nathan and Stokes. 'See, we make progress, an airport.' Malik then looked at the cluster of low buildings and greyish white runways.

'Doesn't seem that there are any aircraft about. What's that over there, by the big brown hangar?' Malik pointed towards a long, thin cylinder shape, that stood on a steel latticework of legs. Several aerials and fins projected from the sides and top of the cylinder and at the rear appeared an attached cluster of long, silver coloured tanks.

'It's the old Hyperion,' Jon answered briefly, as he drove the buggy towards a wide stone bridge that spanned a creek, following a roadway that continued towards the runway area. 'She's not flight worthy now and had to be abandoned,' Jon added.

Malik looked around. 'What the hell is going on, then? I can't see anyone about and this is supposed to be an airport?'

'They were evacuated,' said Jon, as he noticed a white light in the buggy mirror that looked like it was following them.

'Evacuated? What the hell do you mean?' Malik snapped.

'From that,' Jon raised his head and indicated the tube-like craft that Nathan had noticed moments before. It was now approaching at speed and looked much bigger. Suddenly rocket trails shot out from the side of the craft and slammed into the immobile bulk of the Hyperion, causing two massive explosions that broke the craft in two blazing halves.

'Christ alive,' Stokes exclaimed. 'Turn left quick and get into those buildings over there.'

Jon twisted the wheel over and the buggy lurched hard left towards what looked like a warehouse and factory area that lined one side of the creek. Stokes directed Jon to drive towards a long, single storey building, with a portico at the front. Several large wooden double doors on the inside face of the portico were closed, but one was open and Jon drove the buggy towards and through it into the darkness beyond, before slamming on the brakes.

They were in a large, dark room, illuminated only by the light coming in from the open door. They could see numerous wooden racks, some containing what looked like large brown canvas covered bales. A large explosion sounded nearby and shook the ground.

'You.' Malik pointed his gun at Jon. 'Is there any other way out of this place?'

'Looks like they're going for the flight deck first,' said Jon. 'I would assume that they will start landing troops soon when they realise there is no resistance.'

'So, how do we get out of here?' shouted Malik.

'You could go back across the creek and go down to the coast, it's not that far. There will be boats there. They wouldn't have been evacuated.'

'Stokes, take a look out there,' Malik ordered. Stokes nodded and ran towards the open door. Nathan looked at Juno, who had so far maintained a glowering silence.

'Anything you know that could help us out here?'

'No,' Juno snarled back. 'We haven't been here long enough to see much more than you have.'

Nathan leaned against the side of the buggy and watched Stokes at the door for a moment.

'We, is it? I suppose it's your boyfriend that put you up to it all. Well he isn't here now, is he?'

'He's not my boyfriend,' Juno snapped. 'He's a friend, who gave me help when I needed it.' Juno felt a surge of affection for Sam in her mind and wondered where and how he was.

Malik walked towards Stokes and together they peered out of the door. Nathan pulled from his pocket the familiar folded sheet of paper.

'Juno, just sign the bloody thing and I'll square it with Malik. You won't have to go off with him. I swear it.'

Juno gave an incredulous laugh and stared at Nathan. Out of the corner of her eye, Juno could see that Jon was on the other side of the buggy and quietly taking out the grey packs that he'd put into the cargo area, before leaving Maeven's house. He looked up and gave a slight shake of his head. Juno responded with the tiniest wink of her eye and then turned towards Nathan.

'Okay then, since you obviously value this over your safety, I'll sign your damned paper and much good may it do you.'

Nathan looked surprised but said nothing and fumbled in his pocket and drew out a pen. He handed it to Juno, together with the folded paper. Juno made a fuss of opening the paper and smoothing it out to read. Then she managed to drop the pen on the ground. Nathan darted down and scrambled under the buggy for it. Juno glanced over and saw Jon retreating into the gloom, carrying the packs. As Nathan stood up, Juno snatched the pen from his hand and signed where indicated. Nathan grasped the paper with a smile. 'Sensible decision.' He grinned, looking very relieved. 'This will save a lot of trouble.'

'Well, I hope you're happy now that you have what you want. You know Nathan, you haven't wanted me for a long time, if indeed you ever did. You were supposed to take care of me. How on earth did we end up like this?' Juno hoped that her effort to command Nathan's attention had allowed Jon to sneak away.

Nathan held the paper tightly and leaned against the front of the buggy and sighed.

'It's not what I wanted. It's Malik ...' He looked at Malik, standing behind Stokes at the door.

'You could have said no, a long time ago,' said Juno quietly.

'There was so much money to be had,' Nathan explained. 'It was so easy to start with.'

'I know,' said Juno. 'Then I suppose it got harder to refuse. It's not as if we needed the money. You were just greedy and couldn't stop.'

'You were happy to live the lifestyle it brought,' Nathan countered as he waved the paper at Juno before pocketing it.

'Yes, I was,' Juno admitted. 'I didn't know what else to do, until recently when Malik made his play for me. I couldn't take that. It was disgusting and I'm surprised that even you went along with it. Goes to show how much power he had over you.'

Nathan looked a little embarrassed for a moment but straightened up.

'I'm going to tell Malik that you've signed. I'll be able to pay him back. This can all be worked out.'

'Oh, Nathan,' said Juno wearily. 'You can't see it, can you? There is no way back from this.'

16

Leo had carried Sam along with him at great speed into the City and followed the road taken by the buggy. He had transformed back into his human form and now crouched with Sam behind a low stone wall.

'Neat trick, that.' Sam had laughed.

'What trick?' Leo was puzzled for a moment. 'Oh, I see. Carrying you like that called a neat trick? I will remember that expression. It was easier for me to cover this distance like that, rather than in this form. Very tiring though.'

They had then seen the destruction of the Hyperion and watched small Nivar attack craft make several passes over the City, each time firing rockets into the built-up areas.

'We must get to her quickly,' Sam urged. 'Anyway, can you see where they are?'

Leo concentrated. 'I can see three persons in the building over there. See? The long one with the red roof tiles and the portico. You see that open door. They are in there. One other though has left, moved to the rear of the building and is now moving away, towards the centre of the City.'

'Look.' Sam grabbed Leo's arm and pointed to the left. A tall figure had emerged, walking slowly round the side of a building. The figure looked to be clad in some form of black armoured plates and moved in a slow and deliberate fashion, with what looked like a heavy machine gun held out in front. A pale head showed from under a small black helmet that mounted a vision scope and protective goggles.

'What is it?' Sam hissed.

'It's not human,' said Leo. 'It's an advanced assault droid. No thinking ability simply reacts to computer generated orders. They are usually sent in to soak up enemy fire before the real troops come in. That means there must be a Nivar landing party somewhere. Look Sam, there's another one.' Sam followed Leo's pointed finger.

'Looks like they're making towards that building you thought Juno and the rest were in.' Sam jumped up. 'In which case we've got to help.'

'Hold on, Sam. I have an idea.' Leo smiled. 'We don't want to attract any attention from the Nivar, which would endanger Juno.'

Nathan moved up behind Malik, who turned round in surprise. 'Don't creep up on me like that. I might have shot you.' Malik scowled and put his gun away.

'Over there!' Stokes shouted. He pointed at two figures lumbering towards them.

'Fucking hell. Looks like something out of Star Wars.' Stokes raised his gun. 'We can't take them on. Have you seen what they're packing?'

Nathan appeared not to have been listening and drew out the white paper from his pocket.

'Look, Malik, she's signed over the funds to me. I can repay what …'

'Are you bloody mad?' Malik shouted. 'Look out there and see what's coming. Do you think your paper can help now?' He struck the paper from Nathan's hand, and it fluttered out of the doorway and into the street.

Nathan gave a strangled cry and leaped forward to pick up the document. One of the oncoming droids spotted the movement and brought up its weapon.

Nathan stood up, paper in hand, facing Malik with a triumphant grin on his face. At the same moment, a blast from a Nivar weapon took him in the back, ripping open a bloody hole. Nathan died instantly and his body crumpled to the ground. The paper lay in the dust.

Stokes took careful aim and fired two shots at the advancing droid.

The shots hit him on the head and reduced it to a messy pulp. The droid staggered and then sank to its knees, its weapon flamed again and the shot crashed into a nearby building as the thing toppled forward. The remaining droid must have seen what had happened but stood still, weapon held at the ready.

Juno pushed in between Stokes and Malik and screamed at the sight of Nathan's sprawled body, then she saw movement ahead and noticed Sam and Leo some way off. Sam was shouting something and flapping his arms to indicate that she should get down.

Leo stood still as Sam gestured to Juno. Then a pale mist emerged from nowhere and moved quickly towards the general area of Juno and the others. Sam gave Leo a quizzical look. 'That's your idea, then? Mist?'

Leo frowned in concentration, holding his arms out in front of him. The bank of mist rolled forward and wrapped around the remaining droid as it stood by its downed comrade.

'What did you expect?' Leo snapped.

'Big ball of fire? Something like that,' Sam threw back.

'It's not easy,' said Leo. 'The concentration required is intense. It really works better with more than one projecting the image in unison.'

A small explosion ripped through the mist and threw up a pall of light brown smoke and dust that drifted away. Sam ran forward, but couldn't see any sign of Juno, or Malik and his guard.

'Juno!' Sam yelled several times, but there was no response.

Sam couldn't see from his position, three other assault droids advancing. Stokes, however, had a better view and shouted a warning to Malik, who looked desperately about. He now noticed that the building they were in was large and that while there were many wooden racks taking up space, there was sufficient room between them for the buggy to be driven through. Malik whistled to Stokes, who turned his head.

'Stokes, let's get out of here. We'll use the buggy to see if we can find a way out of the back.'

Stokes nodded and with a final glance outside darted back and jumped into the driving seat of the buggy.

Juno also sneaked a look outside, but could see only drifting mist, interspersed with smoke. She thought she might have heard Sam's voice, but it sounded faint and someway off.

In the meantime, Stokes had familiarised himself with the buggy controls and switched on its headlights. As he turned the vehicle round, Malik jumped into the remaining front seat. Juno ran towards the vehicle.

'Wait for me,' she yelled.

Stokes held the speed low, despite Malik's urging to leave her, and as Juno hauled herself into the back Stokes accelerated the buggy rapidly and it sped off through the darkness between the racks. As they pulled off, a large explosion boomed out, demolishing the wooden doors they had stood by moments before and bringing down some of the ceiling. As they raced away, Malik suddenly remembered Jon.

'Where's the guy who drove us here? Where did he creep off to?' Stokes shook his head and concentrated on his driving, as he slewed the buggy round the various lines of racks.

'Bastard's left us to it,' Malik snarled. 'Bet he knows a safe way out.' He glared at Juno hanging onto the sides of the buggy. 'I would have left you behind, but Stokes is soft. I don't owe you anything and if you hold us up … well.' Malik didn't get to make any further threats as a dim light showed up ahead to the left. Another set of wooden double doors came into view. They stood slightly open. Stokes braked hard and the buggy slithered to a halt on the smooth concrete floor.

'Take a look outside,' Malik ordered, as he got out of the buggy, leaving Juno in the back.

Stokes took out his gun and crept forward to peer cautiously between the doors.

'No one in sight, boss. Looks clear to me,' he said

Malik joined Stokes at the doors. 'Well, looks like the airport's out of action. Suppose we try to find someone in charge. There must be someone here who can tell us where it's safe.'

'There's no one,' said Juno. 'Maeven told us that all the people had left the City a couple of weeks ago. They knew this was coming.'

An exasperated Malik pushed a hand through his hair. 'Fuck it all! So here we are, on our own with Darth Vader and his merry men coming to kill us. Wait though.' He narrowed his eyes as he thought and then looked at Juno.

'You must have come here through that weird gate thing, where the stones were. Like us you came through that gate with that Sam. He must have known how to get here.' Malik drew his gun and checked it over. 'In which case you can get us out of this nightmare.'

'But I don't know where we are,' Juno protested. 'Sam and I only got as far as Maeven's house when you found us. We never got as far as this City.'

'You must know how to get from that gate to the house,' Malik countered.

'Vaguely,' Juno replied defensively. 'Sam's been to the beach before and had a fair idea of what he was doing.'

'So, we find this Sam and he tells us the way home,' said Malik with a cunning look on his face. 'I reckon he'll come for you, so all we have to do is use you as the bait.'

Another heavy explosion rocked the building, sending down a shower of white dust from the ceiling.

'How's he supposed to find us in a goddamn war zone?' shouted Juno, anxious that Malik didn't guess how much she had come to care for Sam.

Malik gave a thin smile. 'The main point of contact as I see it must be this Maeven's house. Maybe we ought to return there and you'd better hope that Sam's waiting for you.' Malik turned away from Juno.

'Stokes, change of plan. We've got to get back to that isolated house we first came to. The one where the old lady was, with the creepy guy who was driving the buggy. Looks like the way home may be found there.'

'Okay. It's still clear outside, boss,' Stokes called out.

'Then get the doors open,' said Malik.

Stokes pushed the doors wide open and then froze. 'Boss, ahead. Look, more of those things.'

Four assault droids were marching slowly down the street, weapons held ready.

17

'Get going,' Malik shouted to Stokes. 'Stay here and they'll find us.'

'Which way, boss?' Stokes looked out anxiously at the streets outside.

'Left, go left, but get going,' yelled Malik as he jumped back into the front seat of the buggy. Stokes looked over his shoulder at Juno as she climbed in the back and then drove the buggy at speed out into the sunlight. The assault droids registered the presence of the vehicle and assumed an offensive mode, but Stokes was too fast for them. The buggy careered down a long street, lined with what looked like factories and workshops. Crossing a couple of intersections at speed there did not appear to be any pursuit and no further sign of any assault droids. After a short distance, the street scene gradually changed from an industrial and merchant aspect to one of small, well maintained three storey terraced houses. A little further on, the street widened and tall, green leafed trees provided some shade to the wider stone pavements that now bordered the road. The houses grew grander. Detached properties, often with manicured front gardens, or gated white stone walls that would have screened the occupiers of the big houses from the intrusive glances of passers-by. Still, they saw no one about.

A throbbing sound, much like that of a helicopter caused Juno to look upwards. A little way behind them, what looked like a thin, flat tube, with rotor housings on four corners and a large, covered cockpit at the front. Several thin tubes were suspended beneath the craft. Juno hammered Malik's shoulder and as he turned and scowled at her, she pointed upwards. Malik swore and shouted at Stokes.

'We're being followed. Can you get any more speed out of this thing?'

'Foot's down already,' said Stokes as he hung grimly onto the steering wheel. 'I can't tell what the charge level is so I don't know when it might pack up.'

'Keep it going,' Malik urged as he stared up at the aerial craft. A small puff of white came from one of the tubes and a moment later a small explosion sounded behind them and the front wall of a nearby house disintegrated in a shower of smoke, splintered stone and dust. The pressure wave of the blast rocked the buggy and Stokes started to weave about to try and throw the pilot of the craft off his aim.

The next shot came closer, this time to the right, shaving through the canopy of a tree, showering leaves and torn branches in all directions, before exploding in the garden of a house.

Malik grabbed Stokes' arm. 'Look, up ahead, there's some sort of bridge over the street. Get us under there.'

A great, white stone bridge arched over the street, offering darkened cover from the air pursuit. Stokes slammed on the brakes as the buggy raced under the bridge and they all jumped out and ran further into the shadows. Tall streetlights had evidently provided light under the bridge in normal times but were now all turned off. They could hear the craft hovering overhead, waiting for them to emerge from the cover of the bridge, but it didn't come down any lower to investigate.

'I don't think we've shaken it off,' said Juno. 'I bet it's calling up droids to come in.'

Malik looked about. There appeared to be a ground floor metal door in the bridge structure. The street had widened at that point, as if indicating that it was possible to park a vehicle there and go into some place. In the sunlight ahead, the street gave into a tree lined square faced with tall concrete buildings that looked like offices. There didn't seem to be a continuation of the street beyond.

'Dead end,' fumed Malik.

'We can't go back, or that thing up there will get us,' said Stokes.

Malik walked towards the metal door. It was locked. 'Maybe this will get us out of here, stand back.' He drew his gun and shielding his face shot the door lock with two shots. The door swung inwards to reveal a dark interior, with steps that led upwards.

'Let's try this out,' said Malik. 'We can't stay here.'

'So, can you see where they are?' Sam asked as Leo stood and concentrated, his head in his hands.

'Yes, three of them, some way ahead and to the left.'

'Three, only three of them?' Sam asked anxiously.

'Yes. I am sorry. I can only detect three,' Leo confirmed.

Sam felt a tightening in his stomach. One of them was possibly lost then, or even dead. God forbid that it was Juno. 'We have to get to them,' said Sam. 'Come on.' He ran ahead along the street with Leo following on behind. Fortunately, it was clear of droids.

At one point they had to duck into the shadows afforded by trees at the side of the street as an aerial fighting craft droned overhead.

'They seem to be more over to the right now,' said Leo as he stared skywards.

'Would it help if Perra was here?' Sam suggested. 'To aid with the concentration.'

'Yes of course it would be easier, but I have told her to stay where she is, setting up the fusion bar ready to seal the rent. It's a very delicate instrument and requires careful calibration.'

'Great,' said Sam. 'We're on our own, then. Bear right here?'

Leo nodded and pointed forward and they both raced on towards the City centre.

The steps went upwards and came out in a small hall, with plain, grey plastered walls and a pale wooden door ahead. Stokes leaned against the door and listened for a moment before shaking his head. 'Nothing. Sounds clear.' He gingerly opened the door, gun held at the ready, to reveal a large open area with coloured paving tiles and pastel coloured walls. On one side what looked like a row of wooden doors that might indicate lifts behind. A flight of concrete steps was next to the doors and climbed up and turned.

'They might be lifts,' said Stokes, jerking his thumb towards the doors. 'If the power's off then they won't be working, even if they were we don't want to get stuck inside if there's a problem.'

'Okay,' said Malik. 'We go upstairs and see if we can spot a way out of this place.'

They climbed quietly up the stairs, Stokes leading with his gun in his hand pausing every so often to listen for any sounds. There was the occasional sound of distant explosions, but otherwise the place seemed to Juno to be eerily quiet. At the top of the stairs, Stokes motioned for them to halt and wait until he had a look round. He crept round the wall and after a while returned.

'There's a wide area up here. Looks like a long gallery down one side that looks down on to the City with offices on the other.'

They walked a little way along the gallery and from large windows could see the City stretch away from their position. Up higher the place looked bigger, with buildings of all shapes and sizes. They could roughly make out that the streets seemed to be planned to form something like the spokes of a wheel that converged upon a large central square. In the distance, smoke rose up from several places and a couple of aerial fighting craft flew overhead. They appeared to be quartering the City, looking for signs of opposition.

Walking along the line of the gallery windows, the three came to a corner, where the windows ran on to the left along another wide gallery. Malik stared out of one of the windows and then pointed with his finger. 'See there? In the distance. That looks like that old lady's house, on the rise.'

Juno stood beside him and could just about make out what looked like Maeven's house. 'Yes, it does look like it. If we go down and manage to come out over there,' Juno pointed towards a large open area on top of a large single storey building, 'we ought to be able to get from there and onto that bridge. I think it's the one we came over when we came to the City. We can then get out and head for the house.' Juno noticed several doors along the walled side of the gallery, walked over to one and opened it.

'What are you up to?' Malik asked.

'I need a pee,' said Juno irritably. 'I could also do with a drink.'

'She's right,' said Stokes. 'We should try to remain hydrated.'

'Of course,' said Malik sarcastically. 'Don't wander off, then. You don't want to be left behind.'

'What do you care?' Juno snapped back. 'Nathan explained to me that dirty little scheme of yours for getting off with me.'

'Ah, did he? I wondered whether he'd have the balls to let you know. He did think highly of himself, as I expect you know. However, in the end he was not a clever man, just a greedy one. He really only thought of money. I admit that you did have a certain charm, although to look at you now … well.'

Juno couldn't think of a cutting remark and stalked off through the open door. It led to a large room, with windows down one side of the plain, off white walls. Several desks and chairs and filing cabinets completed the office look. On one side of the room was another wooden door. She walked over and opened it and breathed a sigh of relief as she found the toilet area.

A few minutes later, Juno looked at herself in a wide mirror that stood atop a row of wash basins. The beautiful dress that she had chosen at Maeven's house was looking crumpled and dirty. Her face was smudged and her hair unkempt. 'Can't be helped,' said Juno aloud. An image of Nathan dead, flashed through her mind and was gone in an instant. Then Juno thought of Sam and wondered if he was okay. She turned one of the taps and was pleased to find that some water supply still existed. Washing her hands in the cold water, Juno splashed some on her face and drew her wet fingers through her hair to try and impose some semblance of order. She bent down over the tap and managed a good drink before the water reduced to a trickle and then gave out. Ablutions completed as far as possible, Juno retraced her steps to the gallery and found Stokes staring out of one of the windows.

'We ought to get going before the light fades,' he said quietly. 'We don't want to travel in the dark with those droid things about.'

'True,' Juno agreed. 'Where's his majesty?'

Stokes gave a brief smile. 'Gone further along to see if he could find a way from here down to the bridge.'

'Tell me,' said Juno. 'Why do you work for an asshole like him? You know that all bets are off in a place like this. You could do what you want.'

'Because I pay him a lot of money,' said Malik from behind. He had crept back without making a sound, making Juno jump. 'It's no good you trying to drive a wedge between us, or any crazy psychological tricks. We simply have to get to a certain place and then it's back home. All quite logical. Not sure what the outcome for you will be though,' said Malik with a nasty grin.

'Provided we don't get killed in the meantime,' Juno retorted.

Malik drew his gun and tapped the barrel with his finger. 'Well, we have insurance, don't we? Stokes is a dead shot and I'm not bad either. Come on, I've found another set of stairs, this time going down from this level.'

18

'Look.' Sam pointed excitedly ahead. A buggy had been left by the roadside, under a large bridge. 'Might be the one Maeven had.'

They were soon standing in front of the metal door. 'Looks like the lock's been shot off,' said Sam. 'Wonder if they went up those stairs?'

'Could be,' said Leo. 'I can't concentrate enough to locate them at present, too much distraction and I have a blinding headache. It's not that easy to track people by thinking about them.'

'Okay, I think it's up, then,' said Sam. 'Switch your head off and give it a rest. Everything round here seems to have been left in order when the people went, but this damage to the door looks very recent. Must be Malik, or his mate.' Sam ran up the stairs, with Leo following on and rubbing his temples. They soon found themselves in the open area with the lift doors and the stairs.

Leo and Sam found the gallery and were walking along, looking out of the windows, when Leo stopped suddenly and grabbed Sam's arm. 'See, below, it's them, we've nearly caught up.'

Sam pressed up against the window and stared at the single storey building below. He could clearly see Malik and Stokes running ahead, followed a little way behind by Juno. 'At least she's alive.' Sam breathed thankfully, suddenly aware that he had voiced his thoughts aloud. 'No sign of Nathan then, wonder what happened to him? We must follow them, catch up,' said Sam as he ran along the gallery.

'Sam,' Leo shouted. 'One of those flying machines.' Sam stared as he saw the craft fly towards the building. Stokes must have heard it and shouted a warning. The three of them ran on as hard as they could towards what looked like a box-like structure sited on the roof that served as an access point. It looked as if there were several doors in the box.

The craft settled slowly towards the roof and landed in a small cloud of dust. Immediately four droids clambered out and moved slowly towards the box.

Leo had left Sam anxiously watching the flying machine and the droids. He returned after a little while and said that he had found stairs going down that may well lead to the roof of the building and the others. Sam wanted to charge on down but was also reluctant to leave the sight of Juno tugging open one of the doors on the box. She leaped inside followed by Malik and Stokes. Just at that moment, one of the droids fired his weapon at the box and the resultant explosion blew a small hole in the wall close by the open door. Not hesitating any longer Sam joined Leo and they scuttled as fast as they could down the stairs. They burst out through a doorway and onto the flat roof they had viewed from the gallery windows above. The craft had now gone and there was no one in sight. They immediately ran for the box where Sam had last seen Juno duck into an open door.

The door hung open and they saw steel steps leading downwards. Sam was struck by the emergency style red lighting that enabled them to see ahead. He also sniffed. 'Smells like machine oil, or something like it. Can you hear anything?' Leo listened for a moment and then shook his head.

The steps continued down into the dimly lit depths and they became aware of a large room opening up, containing huge steel tanks with masses of connecting steel pipes and cabling. There were other machines visible that looked like dynamos. A number of racks were stacked high with spare machine parts and lengths of piping. As they reached the concrete floor a sound came from the right. Leo pointed and Sam made to move in the direction indicated.

'Be quiet,' Leo whispered. 'Don't forget that those droids have probably come down here after the others.'

Sam picked up a short length of metal piping from one of the racks and hefted it in his hand. 'Just in case.' He gave a grim smile.

Sam and Leo walked cautiously between more of the dynamos and then Sam raised his hand for them to stop. 'Ahead, see?'

In the reddish gloom they made out one of the droids, standing, weapon ready. Next to it stood a tall figure dressed in a long black cape, with a hood folded behind. The figure was also wearing long black trousers, with a stripe of gold braid down the leg, tucked into knee high black leather boots. They could make out long brown hair flowing over the cape hood and a headphone device that projected forward near the mouth.

'Doesn't look like a droid, more like a living being,' said Sam. 'Perhaps it's some sort of commander. Maybe a superior form of droid.' Before they could do anything, another droid lumbered into view, coming from the left and then moved on behind some red painted tanks held up on steel racks.

There was a sudden crack of a gun and what sounded like a droid returning fire.

Dodging round to the right, Sam and Leo navigated their way swiftly round machinery to try and get beyond the droids. The strategy worked well as they found themselves suddenly in sight of Juno and the others, who were crouched behind a number of metal drums and canvas covered bales.

'Juno,' Sam said, as loud as he dared, but she didn't hear him.

A droid weapon blasted a hole in a bale near to Juno, smoke rose from the burning canvas and she ducked back. Sam saw Stokes rising slightly from behind another bale, gun held at the ready. Malik's head then bobbed up from behind a box close to Juno, staring about as if looking for an exit. Stokes fired his gun at an advancing droid, but it didn't appear to have caused any damage as the droid kept on coming forward. Stokes took steady aim and fired again and hit the droid in the head, smashing it open and spewing greenish liquid about. The droid slumped down to the ground and dropped its weapon. Another droid fired and its shot blasted into a tank to the right of Malik. A sheet of blue flame shot out from the ruptured tank, together with a cloud of dense grey smoke.

Sam moved forward and shouted out Juno's name. This time she heard him, her head turned and a look of astonishment and then joy flashed across her face.

'Get down,' Sam yelled.

At that moment Sam heard Stokes shout to Malik, 'One more, then I'm out.'

He stood slightly higher to get a better view when a shot from a droid weapon ripped open a bloody gash in Stoke's chest and threw him back as if he was a limp rag doll. At the moment he was hit, Stokes had fired his gun. The shot went wide and hit another tank, causing a noxious smelling liquid to spurt out. A droid standing near the damaged tank fired its weapon in Malik's direction. The blast ignited the liquid. An exploding ball of red flame flowed round the droid and it collapsed to the ground in a blazing heap. Sam ran forward to Juno and as he did so, he glanced to his left and saw the droid commander. His black cape held up to shield his face from the heat of the fire. While he was backing away, he saw Sam and started shouting something into the headphone's mouthpiece.

Juno grabbed at Sam as he closed with her and they hugged.

'Christ, we've been looking for you,' said Sam joyfully.

'I'm okay.' Juno smiled briefly. 'God knows how you found me but I'm so glad …' Juno's words were cut short by the boom of an explosion as one of the tanks blew up, causing part of the ceiling to collapse in a fresh wave of heat and smoke.

'We must leave, now,' Leo urged and he beckoned them to follow him.

Malik stood, looking surprised to see Sam and Leo. He was still holding his gun, then he looked down at the body of Stokes and looked shocked. 'Seems we ought to work together,' said Malik evenly. 'Those things will be back soon.' He put his gun away and followed the others as they moved away.

'Where's Jon?' Sam asked as he and Juno ran to keep up with Leo.

'We went into some sort of warehouse after coming into the City, to hide from the droids. They seemed to be everywhere. Jon went off on his own when Malik and Stokes were distracted. I think he had something to do for Maeven.'

Juno paused to catch her breath and then said softly, 'Nathan's dead. So stupid, he was trying to get me to sign over to him some funds that he had put into my name. One of the droids shot him. Can you believe it? Even then he was more concerned about his bloody money. I don't think he had really taken on board was happening and the danger we were in.'

Smoke had begun to fill the space and soon they were all coughing when they reached Leo, who held open a heavy steel door.

'I've had a brief look inside. Looks like more stores and there are some double doors to the right. We can't go back so we'd better get inside quickly and try to go further on.'

Leo hastened them through and then slammed the door shut. A dull rumble behind showed that they had just missed another explosion. They all moved carefully between racks of stores, illuminated by the same red emergency lighting.

A faint sound nearby gave them reason to pause and listen. It sounded like someone shuffling along and coming closer. Malik got out his gun and peered round one of the racks.

'Careful,' said Sam. 'Might be one of those droids.'

'Doesn't sound like it, besides, I think I can hear breathing.' Malik leaped out from behind the rack before Sam could stop him and shouted, 'Freeze.'

Sam almost burst out laughing. In front of them stood the small, thin form of Jon. His black tunic and trousers were torn and dirty, but he was still clutching the two grey packs that he had first loaded into the back of the buggy. Jon's face was grimy and glistened with sweat.

He was also limping and was very surprised and glad to see them.

'So, our friend returns,' Malik mocked, as he put his gun away.

'Let him be,' said Sam. 'Jon, have you seen any of those droids in here?'

'No, but there are many outside. They'll no doubt come in and start searching the buildings.'

'You're limping,' said a concerned Juno. 'Have you been hurt?'

'No, fortunately. I was trying to run across an open space and evade drones when I slipped on the edge of a gutter and fell. I think it's a sprained ankle and my knee hurts, but I can still move.' Jon rubbed his knee and grimaced.

'Where are you heading for, Jon?' Sam asked. Malik began muttering about getting going and leaving Jon behind as he would slow them down.

Juno rounded on Malik. 'We are not leaving Jon behind, so don't even think about it. If you want to piss off on your own and get killed, then please do so.'

Malik was a little taken aback by the vehemence of Juno's outburst.

'He left us in the lurch,' Malik said in a surly tone. 'Why should we care what happens to him?'

'I have to complete the task that Lady Maeven asked of me,' said Jon seriously. 'These are two new firing keys.' He nodded at the grey packages held firmly in his hands. 'I must fit them to enable the missile firing sequence to run properly. The problem I have is that I cannot communicate with Lady Maeven as I lost my device when I fell.'

'What good do you think a few missiles will do?' Malik sneered. 'Have you seen what's going on outside? This place has had it and the best thing we can do is get the hell out. So why are we standing here talking to him?'

'Jon, where do you need to go to install the new keys?' Sam asked, ignoring Malik.

Jon gave a little smile. 'Well, near here. There should be double doors. Could be those over there. It's the entrance to a control room. The idea was to locate it in a warehouse area and so not to attract any attention. Mind you, that was a long time ago.'

'Well, let's get going, Jon,' said Sam.

'I don't believe this,' Malik said.

'You do what you want, Malik,' said Sam forcefully. 'Juno, Leo and I are going to help Jon. This might help all of us if it succeeds.' With that, Sam helped Jon walk towards the doors that Leo had first spotted.

'Bastards,' said Malik under his breath as he looked about the storage room for a way out.

Another muffled explosion sounded back from behind the closed steel door they had come through and this prompted Malik to catch up with the others.

Jon produced a small card and inserted it into a panel to the side of the doors. He glanced at the others and then gently pushed. The doors swung open easily. It was pitch black inside and Jon groped along the interior wall to find a switch. A click and then a light snapped on to reveal a small room, with a large metal desk and a wall panel in front of it. Jon walked over to the desk and found, as he had expected, a number of built in hatches at the back. He flipped them up. Inside were individual clear tubes with wires running through them. Jon quickly pressed a number of switches located on the surface of the desk to activate the wall screen and found that two of the tubes did not display a light.

'This is what Lady Maeven found,' said Jon. He leaned over the desk and extracted one of the dead tubes. Juno handed him one of the grey packages, from which Jon carefully took an identical tube from its protective covering and then inserted it into the vacant slot. Immediately the tube showed a light. The other defective tube was similarly replaced.

'That's it?' said Sam incredulously.

'Yes,' said Jon, as he wiped a hand over his face. 'Simple as that. The problem was getting here to do the job.'

'So, can we now get out of here?' said Malik huffily.

'Just a quick check first,' said Jon. He pulled out a thin metal shelf from under the desk and pressed a small switch located on it. 'Now we shall see,' he said to himself. The wall panel suddenly came to life and displayed a number of graphs and technical tables.

'All is well.' Jon smiled.

'How can you let Maeven know?' Sam asked. 'You said yourself that you had lost your communicator. Can we get a link to Maeven from here?'

'Ordinarily, yes,' said Jon. 'But in normal peacetime situations there was no need to have communications operational within this control hub, but Lady Maeven can in fact activate the missile control remotely from her house. We didn't want an enemy logging into our communications and locate this site too soon.'

'So, Maeven could fire the missiles, via this site, from her house?'

'Yes, the failed firing keys should now show up on Lady Maeven's control panel as having been replaced and now operational. Now I think we should leave here.'

'I don't think we can go back the same way,' said Sam. 'That way's probably been blown to hell by now.'

'There's another way out.' Jon smiled. 'There's always more than one way in and out.' He pressed a button on the desk and a door to the side of the room quietly opened.

'This way.' Jon led them through to a small landing with steel spiral staircase that snaked downwards into the dark. Jon pressed a wall switch and a pale light came on from above to partially illuminate the way down.

'Where does this come out?' Sam asked as they clattered down the staircase.

'In the old police headquarters,' said Jon. 'It's mostly used to store equipment now but I'm hoping there might be a buggy left there that we can use to get out of the City.'

'Then we have to get over the bridge to get back to Maeven's house?' Malik asked. 'That might be easier said than done.'

19

'This is it,' said Jon, as they stood before a metal door. They had filed through a succession of dimly lit pale concrete corridors.

'Beyond this door is the old police vehicle park,' said Jon. The door wasn't locked and he opened it slowly and peered round. 'Looks deserted.' He went through, followed closely by the others.

They found themselves in a large hangar type room, sunlight coming in through thin, tall glass windows showed up a number of brown painted buggies lined up.

'Wow, look at that,' said Sam appreciatively as he walked round a heavy vehicle with an open cab and heavy steel roll bars and struts. There were bench seats in the back. 'Looks like some sort of dune buggy, Look at those big tyres. Good for off road.'

'Fancy yourself in this?' Juno smiled.

'Too true,' Sam answered. 'The ultimate boy's toy.'

Juno rolled her eyes. 'Looks uncomfortable to me.'

Jon leaned in the cab and checked the control panel. 'Still got some charge. I'll connect it up to a fast flow.' He dragged over a cable and connected the vehicle to a nearby wall charger. 'Still operational! Shouldn't take too long and we don't need a full charge, only enough to get back to Lady Maeven's.'

Malik looked towards a large metal roll back door. 'So, what's outside?'

'Small forecourt,' said Jon. 'Then left into the street running up to the main bridge we came in on and then hard right and there you are, straight run beyond.'

'We'll have to go fast.' Sam grinned. 'No telling what droids and flying machines may be about.'

'I take it, Sam, that you're volunteering to drive this thing?' Juno grinned.

'Sure, unless someone else wants a go, hopefully not. Leo you've been very quiet. Can you see a problem?'

'I've been in contact with Perra, letting her know what's going on. The fusion bar is set up in position and is ready to activate. She is concerned about the situation here and wants to join us. I must admit that I could use her ability to fuse with my mind. You know, two heads are better than one.'

'Where's Malik?' said Juno, looking about.

'Over by the door, last time I saw him,' said Sam.

The door had been rolled back just sufficiently to let someone out. Sam ran over and nearly bumped into Malik as he squeezed back through.

'Where the hell did you go?' said Sam angrily. 'We have to stay together.'

'What, are you my fairy godmother?' Malik retorted. 'While you were drooling over playing boy racer I decided to take a little look outside.'

'And?' Sam demanded.

'Just as Jon said. Didn't see anyone or anything. Looks clear to go.'

'Okay then,' said Sam shortly. 'Jon, what's the status on the recharge?'

'Up to sixty per cent,' said Jon, looking at an illuminated wall screen on the charging unit.

'I should think that's enough to get us out of the City.'

Very slowly, Sam pushed the door back. Jon was already sat in the front passenger seat of the buggy, ready to act as a guide. The others piled into the back seats, clinging onto the struts. Jon gave Sam a summary of how the controls worked and then Sam gave a gentle push on the accelerator. The buggy was moving slowly forward out of the building and into the sunshine. Sam looked over his shoulder.

'Keep a good look out for the flying machines.' He noticed that Leo was staring ahead, as if in deep concentration.

'Just follow this road,' said Jon.

Fortunately, the road was not particularly wide and was also bordered by a number of tall buildings, offices and factories. Several leafy trees also stood in a broken line along the roadway and afforded some degree of shading and cover which would make aerial surveillance harder.

The road began to rise and Sam could see the bridge up ahead.

'Top of the rise and turn right,' said Jon. Sam nodded. He was beginning to enjoy driving the big vehicle swiftly and silently onwards. Some greyish smoke rose over buildings to the left, but otherwise there was no sign of the enemy.

Sam had to slow down as the junction came up. He swung round to get on the bridge and immediately slammed on the brakes with a curse. Ahead, four droids stood across the width of the bridge, weapons held ready.

'Bugger me, where did they come from?' Sam swore. He wrenched the steering wheel over and tried to turn to the left but was brought up by the sight of one of the aerial craft, parked up and filling the street. Four more droids stood in front of the craft. To the side lounged a figure.

'He was back in the storeroom. He was the one that looked like a droid commander,' shouted Juno. Sam toyed with the idea of a quick reversal back the way they had come but the figure shook his head and walked slowly forward, beckoning the droids to follow him.

Sam slammed his hands on the steering wheel in frustration as the droids closed in.

'Nothing we can do,' he said bitterly as he looked round at an ashen faced Juno. He was surprised to see that Leo had vanished.

The droid commander continued to walk slowly forward and said something in a guttural tone that they didn't understand. The commander touched the side of his headphone and spoke again. This time they could understand, all too clearly.

'You are my prisoners. There is no way out. You must surrender. I wouldn't like to have to order them to open fire.' He indicated, with a sweep of his arm, the droids that followed him.

'Maybe he wants to negotiate,' suggested Malik quietly. 'I'll talk to him and see what he wants. Perhaps we can come to some arrangement. After all, we don't come from here and whatever's going on is none of our business.'

'Looks like we're in the middle of a war, but go ahead, if you think you can do any good,' said Sam.

'You must all get out of the vehicle,' ordered the commander. They climbed slowly out.

'See, the language translator is a wonderful piece of equipment.' The commander beamed, knowing that he had control of the situation. 'You can understand what I say and will act immediately.'

Sam stared at the commander and took in the thin, pale face and the dead looking black eyes and didn't doubt that the commander was used to being instantly obeyed. Sam moved closer to shield Juno.

'I did not order you to move,' said the commander sharply. 'You will all remain still, while I evaluate this situation.'

'Pompous prick,' Juno muttered.

Malik scowled at her and then faced the commander, with his arms held wide.

'Commander, my name is Malik. I can see that we are in a difficult situation here, but I wonder if I may be allowed to speak to you. I have some information that you will find to be of great interest.'

The commander inclined his head and thought for a moment.

'What information could you possibly have that would be of value to me? Tell me and I might be prepared to let you live. Do not think that you are in a position to bargain with me.'

'Commander, firstly I must tell you that I and these others do not come from here. I mean whatever this place is called.' Malik turned his head to indicate the others with his hand. 'Hey, where's that guy Leo?'

Sam shrugged. 'Never saw him go.' However, Sam noticed a thin white light near the side of the grounded aerial craft and smiled to himself.

A confused Malik turned back to face the commander. 'You see, sir, I and these people have come from another world, through a gap in time or place, or whatever you want to call it. I'm not sure how it works, but let's just say that we have found a way in from another world.'

The commander looked sceptical. 'If this is some kind of game, to delay me, you will be very sorry.'

'No, not at all. I know it sounds ridiculous,' Malik protested. 'We have seen you before. In the room with all the tanks. There was fire and explosions.'

'I recall,' said the commander. 'I recognise you now. Why were you there?'

'Trying to escape from your droids and get back to our own world. I can show you the way.'

'Shut your face, you slimy bastard,' Sam growled.

'So how do you intend to get us out of this? You think you're so smart.' Malik snarled. 'This can ultimately be reduced to a business transaction. We have something that he may well wish to have and in return he will let us out of this.'

'You can't let him know. Think,' said Juno angrily at Malik. 'If those droids could get into our world, can you imagine the disaster that would take place?'

The commander advanced a step. 'A female, I see. You would command a fair price in the slave markets. Cleaned up and prepared, I think the Commandery officers should first be afforded an opportunity of a little leisure activity.'

115

'No chance,' Sam shouted.

'Just what do you think you can do to prevent me from acting as I wish?' the commander asked lightly. 'I think I will have you killed. You look insubordinate.'

'No,' Juno screamed.

At that moment, another Nivar aerial craft flew down and settled on the bridge, blowing a cloud of dust away with its retro fans. A stout man, dressed in a dark blue cape, embroidered with golden representations of fantastical creatures alighted and strode towards the gathering. He stared at them all for a moment from deep set brown eyes, as he adjusted the cape and smoothed down his dark blue uniform. He rubbed a pudgy, pale hand over his round, ruddy face.

'Commander Zuris,' said the newcomer in a cold tone. 'We have been monitoring your, ah, discussions with these prisoners. I do hope that you were not intending to take any action upon your own account. You know the protocol. All prisoners to be taken for interrogation by the security detail.'

Commander Zuris could not keep a sneer from his lip. 'Guard Commander Lucatch. Welcome. As you can see this City is completely under our control.'

'Not a difficult task, Zuris, given that there was no opposition,' Lucatch retorted.

'Well, there was some resistance encountered.' Zuris pointed towards Sam and the others. 'A number of droids were destroyed, but we have killed two of their party and captured these as they tried to escape.'

Lucatch nodded. 'Send for a security detail to interrogate them, save for him,' he indicated Malik. 'Then have them eliminated. I want everything settled and dealt with before the High Lord himself arrives.'

Zuris's eyes widened. 'The High Lord is coming here?'

Lucatch could not conceal a look of triumph on his face. 'I

thought you would have known, given your connection to the High Lord's Brethren.'

Zuris's face assumed an immediate bland mask. 'My grandfather is, as you know, one of the High Lord's close companions, but he does not see fit to keep me informed of the High Lord's whereabouts.'

'No, indeed, Zuris,' said Lucatch. He leaned closer towards Zuris and looked carefully at him. 'I would not allege that you have been sniffing dremweed on active duty, but I can see that the colour of your eyes betrays you. It is not something that I will tolerate and I cannot think that your grandfather would approve.' He turned towards Malik. 'You will come with me. I want to hear more about this other world business that you mentioned.'

Sam smiled as Malik and Lucatch walked towards the second aerial craft. Zuris frowned. 'What do you find to amuse you? I can assure you that the security detail will soon wipe out any desire to laugh from your face, or what will be left of it when they have finished.'

'It's just that bastard Malik was being economical with the truth.'

'How so?' Zuris asked quietly as he pressed a tiny switch on his headphone. 'Now we can have a private conversation.'

'Malik doesn't know where the connection to this world from ours is located. He came here in the dark and has no idea how he got here. Now, Juno here and I came in the daylight and know where to go.'

Zuris gave a thin smile as he watched Malik and Lucatch climb into the aerial craft.

'Don't you think you ought to tell your boss?' Sam enquired, with an air of innocence.

'No …' Zuris drawled. 'I think that it might be best to eventually let Lucatch squirm in front of the High Lord, but I will let my grandfather know.' Zuris turned towards Sam, a hard look on his face.

'Don't assume familiarity with me. I can extract the information I want from you and the female at any time.'

Zuris moved towards his droids and indicated that they should re-enter the remaining aerial craft.

'You two go with the droids,' Zuris barked at Sam and Jon.

'What about Juno?' Sam shouted.

'I think a little advanced interrogation is called for,' Zuris said with a lascivious smile. He grabbed both of Juno's arms and dragged her, kicking and swearing round the back of the craft.

Sam tried to intercede but was clubbed to the ground by the butt of a droid weapon before being hustled into the craft.

Zuris looked about and saw a single storey building nearby, with a door wide open to the street.

'Here, I think. A little privacy is called for.' Juno struggled furiously and Zuris, losing patience let go of one of her arms and swiftly punched her hard on the side of her head. Juno doubled up gasping as Zuris then hauled her towards the doorway. He failed to notice that two white lights shone on either side of the door.

20

Zuris pushed Juno through the door and she fell back onto a dusty concrete floor.

'Sam,' Juno yelled as she scrabbled on the ground back towards a bare wall. She glanced round and saw nothing to hide behind or anything that would serve as a weapon to defend herself with.

'He cannot help you now,' said Zuris with a smile. Then he pulled something from an inside pocket of his cape. Juno looked in horror as Zuris held a small length of steel chain and proceeded to wrap it round one of his fists.

'First, a little lesson in discipline I think.' He advanced slowly, eyes fixed on Juno's frightened face, clearly savouring the moment. Suddenly, Zuris twisted about violently, arms flailing. He cursed and cried out, staggering about the room. From behind Zuris Leo appeared and beckoned to Juno. 'Get up, quickly now. Perra is causing him to see nothing but blackness.' Juno needed no second bidding and ran out of the room.

'Get over by the buggy,' said Leo. 'Hide behind so you can't be seen from the craft.' Juno raced off.

Inside the control compartment of the Nivar craft, the pilot was sweating in his flight suit. The controls were not responding and there had just been an order on the comms link ordering all craft to re-embark and take off to rendezvous with the High Lord's craft, the Battle Destructor, but the pilot had a problem.

Zuris suddenly found that he could see. Breathing heavily and scared by the loss of vision, he took in the empty room and stumbled outside, full of rage and fear. He roundly cursed Juno. He thought of what he would do to her when he caught her, but she was nowhere to be seen. She surely couldn't have run that far, that fast. As he stood in the middle of the road he heard the pilot of the aerial craft calling from a hatch in the craft's control section.

'Commander, we have been ordered to join with the other assault craft and rendezvous with the Battle Destructor. The High Lord is near.'

'Now?' Zuris yelled back. 'The High Lord is coming now?' So, Lucatch wasn't lying after all. He clenched his fist angrily. Damn the woman, there was no time to search for her. He must get to the High Lord before Lucatch got his tale in first.

Zuris ran to the craft and ordered the pilot to get airborne immediately.

'There is … ah a … difficulty.' The pilot looked fearful, expecting a raging outburst from Zuris.

'The control panel. Nothing is shown as working. See here. I have sequenced all controls, but nothing. The rotors just refuse to operate and for no reason.'

Zuris swore profusely and then glimpsed back through a viewing panel in the bulkhead. Inside the troop compartment the droids were seated forward in shut down mode and beyond them Zuris could see the one he assumed was called Sam and the other, small man, sitting dejectedly. No, they couldn't have caused this. Zuris cursed the pilot and demanded that he repeat the take off procedure. While being engrossed with the control panel, neither Zuris, nor the pilot noticed a white light appear next to the rear entry hatch and a tall, female figure clad in a shimmering green gold dress suddenly appear. Perra put a finger to her mouth and beckoned an astonished Sam and Jon to come out through the hatch.

'Don't worry about the officer and the pilot.' Perra smiled and whispered, 'They think the controls are not working and are in a panic. They are seeing what I want them to see, but it is not real.'

'The bastard took Juno,' said Sam anxiously. 'I have to find her.'

'Do not worry, Sam.' Perra smiled. 'Leo helped her escape. Juno is hiding behind the dune buggy on the bridge.'

'How did he get her away?' Sam asked, mightily relieved to hear that Junio was safe.

'I gave Zuris a fright by blacking out his sight.' Perra laughed. 'Now, quickly, go and hide behind the buggy with Juno. I will release the pilot and Zuris from their visions and no doubt they will wish to launch.'

Zuris was in such a desperate rage that he was within an ace of battering the control panel with his fist when the lights suddenly came on and the control sequences hit in.

The pilot slumped down in his seat in relief. 'I cannot account for it, Commander. The controls simply did not respond.'

'Never mind that now,' Zuris snarled. 'It's working. Get this piece of shit skywards as fast as you can.'

Sam, Juno and Jon crouched down as low as they could beside the side of the dune buggy. Leo and Perra knelt with them.

'Where's Malik?' Leo asked.

'That piece of work tried to sell us out,' said Sam. 'He was claiming to the main guy in charge that he could show him a way into another world from here. The officer looked dubious to say the least, but then he took Malik off with him in one of those aerial craft a little while earlier.'

The downdraft from Zuris's craft scattered dust about them as it rose. It banked hard and climbed steeply into the sky.

They all jumped back into the buggy. 'Back to Maeven's house,' said Sam.

'I must confirm with Lady Maeven that the missile keys are all working,' said Jon seriously.

'Hang on, then.' Sam grinned as he turned the wheel and pressed down hard on the accelerator. The buggy shot forward and they charged over the bridge.

'Look at that,' said Juno, hanging onto a strut and pointing upwards. They looked up, save for Sam who was concentrating on his driving. About twenty plus of the Nivar aerial craft had risen to form a compact formation. They hovered for a moment over the City, which had been damaged in places, with thick smoke spiralling up. None of the craft seemed to have noticed the dune buggy speeding over the bridge.

Juno gave a cry that surprised Sam, causing him to swerve before regaining control. 'What is it?' Sam yelled.

'Higher up.' Juno pointed, craning her neck backwards. They looked upwards and could make out an enormous vessel descending out of the heavens. A great ship that, to Juno, looked like some Gothic cathedral laid on its side. As it came lower, they could see what looked like great buttresses ranged along the side. A myriad of pipes, tanks and projections lined the upper works. A huge opaque, round panel high up on the front looked like a magnificent glass window and presumably served as part of the main control deck. The smaller aerial crafts climbed higher towards the great vessel, from which a number of large hatches opened upwards to allow them to enter and dock. The army had returned to its High Lord.

21

'What's happening?' Sam asked as they were all bumped around in the buggy that was now racing along a rough track. The built-up area of the City had rapidly given way to grassland and Sam thought he could see Maeven's house in the distance.

'Looks like all the aerial craft have gone back on board the main one,' shouted Juno as she stared upwards. 'It's massive.'

'What's it doing?' said Sam.

'Seems to be moving slowly round, circling the City,' said Leo. 'I don't think they've seen us. Probably too small to notice.'

'That's something,' said Sam grimly.

'It's coming lower,' shouted Juno. 'Bloody hell.'

'What is it?' Sam tried to look round and missed a pothole in the track that sent the buggy bucking and swerving. Sam wrestled with the wheel to regain control, but he didn't slow down.

'It's shot something into the City,' said Leo. 'A missile of sorts. It's hit down near the bridge. There's a lot of smoke.'

Another missile shot from the Battle Destructor and slammed into the defenceless City, causing a huge explosion and clouds of dense black smoke.

'They'll just circle round and destroy the City at leisure,' said Juno sadly, unable to take her eyes from the scene.

It was not many more minutes before Sam braked hard, scattering stones and dust and slewed the buggy round to a stop in front of Maeven's house. Maeven herself ran out as they climbed from the buggy, her once braided hair now flying wildly in an increasing breeze that blew in from the sea.

'I'm so thankful to see you all.' Her eyes ran anxiously over the party. 'But some are not with you?'

'No,' said Sam. 'Two are dead and one traitor has gone off with the enemy.'

'Lady Maeven,' Jon interrupted. 'The new firing keys have been installed but I was unable to confirm this with you as I had lost my communicator.'

'It's not a problem, Jon. I could see on my portable control that the keys are now operational. I was holding on to see you return.' Maeven suddenly looked tired; her eyes filled with tears.

'Dear Jon, I couldn't bear the thought of you not coming home.'

Jon shuffled his feet and looked at the ground. 'It has always been an honour and my great pleasure to have been of service to you and Lord Valeran,' he muttered, face reddening.

'Not just of service, Jon, my dear friend,' said Maeven, as a tear rolled down her cheek. 'Always more than that.' She extended her hand and took one of Jon's hands. 'It is so good to see you here again.'

Sam looked aside to see Leo and Perra in their human form standing closely together, smiling at each other. He glanced at Juno, who leaned back against the buggy, grinning. 'I never thought we'd get out of there alive.'

'Helluva ride.'

A movement out of the corner of Sam's eye made him look up.

'Christ's sake,' he exclaimed. The others looked upwards in the direction Sam was facing. The Battle Destructor had completed a circuit over the City and was now moving in their direction.

'Leo,' said Sam, with alarm beginning to show in his voice. 'Have you anything you can do against that thing? Sort of holy thunderbolt would be good.'

Leo shook his head. 'We are forbidden to take life and in any event the craft is too big for the two of us to deal with.'

'Not even a huge cloud to cover us here?' Sam pleaded.

'Couldn't keep it up long enough,' said Perra. 'Besides, I dare say they have the ability to detect us through any cloud we could generate and fire at us accordingly.'

'What about the missiles? All that we did to get the firing keys in place. Must have been worth it?' Juno asked. She looked about for Maeven, who had run back into the house.

'Lady Maeven has gone to obtain the fire control,' said Jon gravely.

They stood in silence, watching the huge bulk of the Battle Destructor draw near. Maeven suddenly ran out and breathlessly tapped on a handheld pad.

'Sequence confirmed,' she cried out. 'Launch in one, two … now!'

Beyond the City, six plumes of white vapour trailed into the sky as the warheads ascended towards the Battle Destructor. They all stood, transfixed, hardly daring to breathe as the plumes seemed to move with agonising slowness. Suddenly, trails of yellow fire erupted from various points along the sides of the Battle Destructor, each one unerringly took out an incoming missile with a sheet of flame and debris.

'Oh no,' cried Maeven, her arms hanging limply by her sides. 'That was our last hope.'

The bulk of the Battle Destructor advanced and shaded the sunlight from the ground. They could do no more than stand there and wait for the inevitable outcome. Sam turned to Leo and Perra, as he reached for Juno's hand. 'This is not your fight. You can go and do your thing and go back into light. No need for you to stay.'

Leo looked stricken and was about to say something when Jon shouted out excitedly.

'One of the missiles hasn't fired. I saw six launch, but there were seven.'

'He's right,' said Maeven. 'How could I forget? The last one must be one of the old Icarian X models, over one hundred years old but always well maintained. I'll try again.'

Maeven looked at her pad and pressed a couple of buttons.

'Please, please,' she begged. As if in response, a thick plume of grey smoke erupted from a silo near the coastline. A large missile streaked into the sky. The Battle Destructor was now too low, moving too slowly and intent upon what was in front on the ground.

On board, alarms shrieked out. Counter battery fire was being computed but the heavy missile had only a short run to make and it ripped straight into the underbelly of the Battle Destructor, before exploding in a spectacular red and yellow fireball.

For a few seconds, it looked as if the Battle Destructor would absorb the hit and carry on. The watchers on the ground could not see fire blasting through decks and bulkheads, vaporising crew members as they tried to contain the conflagration.

Fire lanced through pipework and fuel tanks and seared into munitions stores. Silent, unheeding, droids were blasted into shards, while their masters twisted and screamed out the last moments of their lives in an effort to escape. A series of large explosions took place internally, blasting parts of the craft apart. It lurched sharply to the left, trailing a huge plume of black smoke from the point of the missile impact. Burning chunks of wreckage fell from the Battle Destructor onto the land, setting grass on fire as the ship, sinking slowly, crossed the coastline and flew, now out of control, over the sea. A great ball of fire blew the control deck apart and finally engines and rotors ceased to function as flame bellowed along the decks of the whole length of the ship. A final gasp, one of the smaller aerial craft managed to lift out of one of the hangars just before it erupted in flame but was caught by a collapsing gantry and smashed in two before it could move away. The flaming, mangled wreck of the once mighty ship crashed into the sea in an enormous wave of smoke and flame. One last fireball flared out from the clouds of steam and the Battle Destructor had gone, leaving only a mass of blackened wreckage littering the water.

Sam hugged Juno and together they jumped for joy in disbelief at what they had just witnessed, having been expecting to be living their last few moments.

Maeven thoroughly embarrassed Jon by hugging him, while Leo and Perra looked out in amazement at the final scene of the catastrophe.

'It appears there are no survivors,' said Leo seriously.

'If they hadn't come here to destroy then they wouldn't have lost their lives.' Maeven laughed. 'The High Lord is gone and the Nivar, as a force have been destroyed. The City has been saved. I will signal the people and they will return. The damage can be repaired and life can begin again.'

'I think Malik was on board that Nivar ship,' said Sam quietly to Juno, still holding her hand. 'They've all gone now. No need to be afraid ever again.'

'No,' whispered Juno. 'I can't believe it. All seemed so certain. My fate unavoidable and then of all things, the late firing of an antique missile alters the whole situation.'

Sam saw Leo and Perra looking at them. 'What is it?' Juno asked.

'Sam and Juno,' said Leo, a little formally. 'Perra and I did come here to close a rent in the dimension between your world and this one. It is time for this to be done.'

22

They all stood still for a moment, taking in what Leo had said. Sam looked across the sea at the pall of smoke that was beginning to drift away, leaving little evidence floating on the water of the carnage that had just taken place. He looked at Juno and suddenly felt a jolt of sadness. What would happen next? He had forgotten that he had a life in the other world, as did Juno. They had been thrown together in this mad escapade and the thought that his and her reality in their world might not be sufficient to keep them together filled him with dread. He wanted to stay in this new world with Juno and forget their pasts.

Maeven came forward and took hold of one of each of Sam and Juno's hands.

'Such a short time you have been here and I have had no time to come to know you both. However, I do know, especially from Jon, that you have both helped save the City and this world and for that I and all the people of the City, who can now return, owe you a debt that cannot be repaid. It is a sadness that at this moment of deliverance and safety that you must be called back to your worlds. We should have had time for celebration, but I see that time does not permit.' Maeven took two delicate golden chains from round her neck. Attached to each was a small golden disc that bore a stylised depiction of the City under a rising sun, with an inscription in tiny lettering round the edge.

'Take these as a small remembrance of the City,' said Maeven as she placed them in Sam and Juno's hands. 'They are very old and represent the seal of the City and were worn by my husband and I when we were Grand Councillors. They are my most valuable possessions and are given with my love.' Maeven then gave Sam and

Juno a long hug in turn.

'Thank you, Maeven,' said Sam solemnly. 'This is a great honour that you have conferred upon us. We'll never forget our time here. It's a great pity that we couldn't stay longer and come to know you and this world better.'

'Can I ask what the words on the seal mean?' asked Juno, looking a little tearful.

'Strength and Happiness to All,' Maeven replied with a smile. 'I wish the same to you both.'

Leo indicated that it was time to go. Sam shook Jon's hand firmly. Juno hesitated, then gave Jon a hug, to his happy surprise.

Leo and Perra led the way back through the dunes and as they walked Sam and Juno stopped and turned to gaze one last time at Maeven's house, where Maeven and Jon still stood. They both raised their arms and Sam and Juno responded with their own salute and then turned to walk on.

Leo obviously knew the way to the location of the rent and it didn't seem to take too long before they found themselves back at the path between the banks of sand, shaded by the deep growths of Marram grass.

Perra had walked slightly ahead and now stood in front of a tall metal rod, about four feet in height, that stood upon four slender metal legs planted firmly in the sand. Perra touched the rod and a pale blue light seemed to emanate and flow round it in a circular motion.

'It is ready,' said Perra. Leo nodded.

'All you must do is go forward. Perra and I will connect physically with the fusion bar, which will then vastly amplify our joint thoughts. This will seal the rent shut.'

Leo stood still for a moment and appeared at a loss for words.

'What we have done. What we have seen, Perra and I. These things we have never done before.' He turned to Perra and held out a hand, she smiled and grasped it. 'We have led such a life together, through endless ages, for the most part acting quietly and unseen and yet, in this form,' Leo passed a hand over his chest, 'in this body, I can say that it has been an experience I will never forget.' Leo faced Perra. 'To touch, to have physical being, it has been so long forgotten. It has been truly wonderful.'

'It need not be forgotten again.' Perra smiled and then bowed her head forward and kissed Leo on the lips.

'Goodbye, Sam and Juno,' said Leo, as he laid his hands on their shoulders. 'I, rather Perra and I, have gained a great deal from your company. It is an honour and pleasure to know you.'

'The pleasure is ours as well,' said Sam unevenly as he clasped Leo's arm in a firm grip. 'Without your help and that of Perra, Juno and I would not have survived here. We cannot give you thanks enough.'

Juno embraced Leo and Perra and then stepped back.

'Will we ever see you both again?'

'Who knows?' Leo smiled. 'Anything is possible.'

Standing with Perra they linked hands and then held them over the glowing rod. Sam shut his eyes at a sudden flash of brilliant white light and they were back inside the dolmen.

23

Juno pushed open the metal gate and they walked slowly out into the dappled shade afforded by the oak trees. The sun was beginning to drop towards the west, sending out golden rays.

'Any idea what day it is?' Juno asked.

Sam patted his trouser pockets. 'Sorry, no idea. Must have lost my phone some time ago.' Juno just shrugged and together they began to cross the field towards Glebe Cottage. They said nothing for a while as their feet swished through the grass, then Juno stopped and faced Sam.

'How do you feel?'

'Strange,' said Sam. 'To be here, now. Did all that really happen?'

'Yes, I understand,' said Juno slowly. 'I know that it's happened. If nothing else look at the state of us.' Juno gave a little smile and then placed the chain and disc that Maeven had given her round her neck. Sam held his chain and then placed it round his neck. 'At least I have proof of what we have seen and done,' said Juno as she looked down at the disc.

'It's been incredible, Sam. I've never felt so scared in my life and yet … so alive. Is that odd?'

'I understand what you feel. But how do we come down from this? I'd have loved to have stayed longer, to see what would happen to the City and whether the people would come back. I would love to have had a long talk with Maeven, well, about everything.'

'Leo and Perra too,' said Juno. 'Their existences are almost beyond belief. They would have had so much to tell us.'

Just before they were to pass through the hedge and into the garden of Glebe Cottage, Juno stopped and burst into tears. Sam was astonished and worried at her outburst. He wrapped his arms round her and held her tight as her body heaved and her tears flowed.

'It's so silly,' Juno gulped. 'Crying like this. I don't know why I'm doing it. I'm not sad or ill, or anything bad.'

'Maybe it's a release of tension,' suggested Sam. 'It wouldn't be surprising after all you've gone through.'

'Yes, you're probably right.' Juno sniffed and wiped away tears from her face with a grimy hand.

'After all, I've been shot at, punched, assaulted, terrified and in fear of my life. You certainly know how to show a girl a good time, Sam.'

Sam laughed loudly as they entered the garden.

'I feel dirty and lousy,' said Juno. 'I could do with a long hot shower and a hair wash. I could probably lose pounds if I had a good wash.'

'Water is programmed to come on twice a day so I suppose there should be enough. Hungry?'

'Odd, but no,' said Juno. 'I do feel very tired, all of a sudden.'

'Me too. Must be all the fresh air and exercise we've had.' Sam smiled.

Juno quickly showered and washed her hair, while Sam prowled round the cottage, looking to familiarise himself with all the items of furniture and other effects, as if trying to assure himself that he really was back in this world. He felt restless, unable to sit or stand and wandered out into the garden. He saw that the lawn needed a trim but didn't feel like doing it. He couldn't think of settling to do something so ordinary. Instead, he turned to look at the sunlight on Anwin Hill. A V shaped formation of what Sam thought might be geese, flew high overhead and he wondered whether they were headed for the great reservoir a few miles away. After a long while of simply staring into the distance and thinking of nothing Sam came to and went back inside the cottage. There was no sound of Juno and he felt momentarily worried. He ran up the stairs. The bathroom was empty. Looking into the main bedroom, Juno was tucked up on the bed, wrapped in blankets. As he drew near Sam could see that she was fast asleep and he then relaxed and smiled to himself.

Still unable to settle, Sam picked up Juno's once lovely dress, where she had dropped it on the floor. He selected some clean clothes for himself from a wardrobe and went to have shower.

Later, Sam put Juno's grubby dress and his dirty clothes into the washing machine and selected a programme. He watched the clothes tumbling in the water for a while and then went to the kitchen and opened a tin of oxtail soup, poured it into a glass bowl and then set it to heat in the microwave.

As Sam sipped the hot liquid, he was conscious that he was performing normal, everyday activities. It was almost as if he was watching himself re-adjust to this reality. He remembered how he had enjoyed driving the big dune buggy and smiled. Then the moment when the missile had torn into the Battle Destructor and that they had, at the last moment, all been saved from certain death. Maeven, Jon, Leo and Perra. People they had come to know and had lived life with at an intense pace, now suddenly gone. Feeling weary, Sam went into the living room. Shadows lengthened as the sun sank. He didn't turn on the TV, not wishing to disturb Juno. His head lolled back against the comfortable chair and he was soon asleep.

Next morning, Sam woke with a stale taste in his mouth and a crick in his neck. He stood up stiffly and stretched. There was no sound from upstairs, so Sam went out into the garden, blinking at the bright sunlight. He wandered round to the front of the cottage and looked over the hedge. There was a large black car parked outside.

As Sam went back inside, he met Juno coming down the stairs, dressed only in an oversize blue denim shirt of Sam's.

'Morning, found this in the wardrobe, my dress has gone. Hope it's okay to use the shirt.' Juno yawned loudly and rubbed her face.

'Sure, your dress went in the wash. I must put it out on the line in a minute. Hungry?'

Juno shook her head. 'Not yet, maybe later. That was a great night's sleep, although I still feel quite tired.'

'There's a big black Mercedes parked outside in the road,' said Sam. 'I suppose it has something to do with Malik. I'm wondering what to do about it.'

Juno groaned. 'No Sam, not yet. There's time enough for all of that. I just need a little time, some more of fantasy land. What did we call it when we were at the beach? Crusoe Land?'

Sam nodded and smiled. 'Good idea.' He had no wish to bring up the subject of Nathan and Malik. Juno was right, a little longer in Crusoe Land would be wonderful.

'Looks like a lovely day outside,' said Juno. She picked up a large throw off the sofa and a fluffy multi coloured blanket. Putting the two under one arm, Juno then picked up two cushions and walked towards the garden.

'Couple of drinks please?' Juno smiled as she went out.

Sam made up some elderflower in glasses and then went out into the garden. Juno had spread the blanket and throw on the grass and was setting the two cushions together. She knelt on the blanket and smiled up at Sam as he approached with the drinks and set them down on a nearby flat stone.

'You okay?' Sam asked.

Juno nodded. 'Sam, can I ask you something?'

'Sure,' Sam replied with a stab of fear in his stomach. If Juno left, for him there could never be any more Crusoe Land.

Juno stretched out on the blanket. 'Can I stay here please, with you? It's where I want to be. Never again at Burton House.'

Relief surged through Sam at her words.

Sam knelt beside Juno. 'It would be the most wonderful thing possible for me if you would stay here forever.'

'I was hoping you'd say that.' Juno laughed. Then she gave Sam an arch smile and proceeded to slowly undo the buttons of her shirt, which she spread open and shook off.

'Do you like what you see, Sam? God that sounded corny.' Juno laughed loudly.

Sam gazed longingly upon the slim body in the warm sunshine and the loving smile on Juno's face. He saw the chain and the disc that sat on her chest.

'Very much indeed,' said Sam softly as he bent to kiss Juno's forehead. She placed a hand gently on his neck and pulled him down upon her.